MOJAVE

Other books by C. Jack Lewis:

Face Down
Manhunter
Renegade Canyon

The *Charlie Cougar Mystery* Series
Double Cross
The Scarlet Canary
The Coffin Racers

MOJAVE

•

C. Jack Lewis

AVALON BOOKS
NEW YORK

Library of Congress Catalog Card Number: 2003095463
ISBN 0-8034-9641-9

Published by Thomas Bouregy & Co., Inc.
160 Madison Avenue, New York, NY 10016

PRINTED IN THE UNITED STATES OF AMERICA
ON ACID-FREE PAPER
BY HADDON CRAFTSMEN, BLOOMSBURG, PENNSYLVANIA

This book is dedicated to my stepson, Zachery J.O. Gilbert, who has managed to turn darkness into light for himself and many of those around him.

The facts stated in the prologue of this book are primarily true. There was a red camel with a skeleton in Union uniform tied to its back; the Confederacy did attempt to start its own camel corps in the early days of the War Between the States; Jefferson Davis did pioneer the use of camels in the Great American Desert during his tenure as Secretary of War prior to Secession and his assuming the office of President of the Confederacy. Reference also is made to other historical figures of the period, as well as sites of forts.

Beyond the references mentioned above, this volume is a work of fiction; any similarity to persons, places, and incidents is coincidental.

Prologue

When the Mojave County *Miner* first started printing those stories about the big camel they'd started calling the Red Ghost, a lot of readers must have thought the newspaper editor was either drunk or trying to insult their minds. Even when the stories were run in the Tombstone *Epitaph* and the Phoenix *Gazette*, most folks didn't take them seriously at all. They tended to think it was more of that fiction writing that had made heroes out of Buffalo Bill and Wild Bill Hickok, more imagination than downright provable truth.

You probably can't blame them much. But Arizona is filling up with folks from the East and, right now, in 1893, they don't know how it was in this desert country thirty years ago. They tend to look at life the way it is now, the railroad sending trains through every day or so, the Apaches held on their reservations, and they tend to figure the West wasn't near so wild as some of them writers like to claim it was.

Fact of the matter is, I'd probably gotten to be some like them. Not that I'd forgotten the red camel. That wasn't likely to happen ever for me, but he'd for certain worked his way into the back of my memory until about ten years back, when I read that first newspaper column about how he had been seen off and on in the Yuma sand dunes. There had been other reports after that of how the beast sometimes rampaged through camps and settlements. Then back about 1883, he killed a woman down around Eagle Creek. She'd gone to fetch some water and they'd found her body later, where it had just about been stomped into the ground. The coroner in Solomon was mighty suspicious at first, figuring she'd maybe been killed by some of her own family. But the creek around her had the marks of big cloven hooves twice the size of those for a horse and there was some red hair caught on a twig where the camel had taken off through the brush. That coroner finally settled for calling it "death in an unknown manner."

Later on, some prospectors said they'd seen the camel and how he had something that looked like a human body tied to his back with rawhide ropes. The camel was a good piece off, but they took a shot at him. They seemed not to have hit him, for he ran off, but when they got up to where the camel had been, they found a human skull on the ground. It still had tatters of hair and sun-dried flesh on it. Folks no doubt would've wondered what kind of mescal they'd been drinking, but them boys brought that skull to town as their proof.

That was about the time I bought the Desert House in Phoenix. I've been running it ever since with a fair amount of luck at keeping my rooms filled, but I didn't always have it so fine. After the War Between the States, I was discharged and had to do a passel of things just to keep eating.

I was a deputy sheriff for a time, then I punched a lot of cows, worked on the railroad one summer, and even did some prospecting. A few times, I tried to tell folks about Big Red and what had happened to us out there in the desert sand, but they all sort of looked at me like I'd stayed too long in the sun. After a while, I didn't talk about it anymore. It's tough to get a prospecting grubstake, when everyone thinks you're either daft or practicing to be the world's champion liar.

But after that report about the red camel being seen, then them prospectors finding the skull, there was all sorts of talk and theories for a few weeks about how that man come to be tied on the camel's back, if it really was so. One theory was that the Apaches had captured the camel in the desert years back. They'd tortured some settler till he was near dead, then they'd thought it good sport to tie him on the beast's back and drive the animal with its burden out into the desert.

It probably wasn't a bad theory as that sort of thing goes, but them that came up with it don't know much about Apaches. Had they ever caught that camel, they'd have butchered him on the spot and eaten him.

But the theory does have some truth around the edges. What really happened was so long ago, I'm sort of reluctant to talk about it. As old as I'm getting, it'd be easy to call me crazy if I tried to tell folks again what really happened.

Chapter One

Thurlow sat in the shade of a manzanita, watching the men gathered around the early morning campfire a few yards away. He didn't like them and he was reasonably sure they thought him some sort of a fool. But he had been sent here to carry out a mission and he would see that it was done, no matter what.

The four camels they had captured already were lined out and ready to travel, when Todd Dixon came over to hunker down beside him. The renegade, like the others, needed a shave, and as he turned his head to look at Thurlow, the latter smelled the bad breath that was a combination of liquor and rotting food.

"I still think we oughta find a box canyon and hold 'em till we get some more," Dixon growled. "It's a long way back to Texas from here. It'll take my men a good three weeks to a month before they kin get back here."

Thurlow glanced away, trying to avoid the stink of the man's breath. Dixon claimed to be one of Quantrill's men, but the younger man had his doubts. If Dixon had ever had any military training, it certainly didn't show.

"They want those camels in Fort Davis. Besides, if we

wait to capture more, the blue coats could catch up to us and we'd have nothing," Thurlow told him. "You're being paid well enough to get them there."

Dixon hesitated for a moment, then nodded his head and stood to shout to the two men, both mounted on horses, who had been assigned to deliver the camels. "Move 'em out!" he called. "But get your tails back here as fast as you can!"

Dixon's hand went to settle on the odd-looking handgun slung in a cutaway holster on his right hip. The holster obviously had been made to hold and protect a smaller gun, and sections had been cut out of the leather so the LeMatt would ride securely, yet be easy to draw.

When he had first seen the revolver, Thurlow had expressed interest and the renegade had allowed him to look at it, but not to handle it. However, the Confederate officer knew a good deal about the strange two-barrel revolver that had been invented in New Orleans by a physician, Doctor Jean Alexander Francois LeMatt.

The doctor, unable to interest anyone in making the gun in the United States, had taken his patents to France, where the first production had been released for European sale in 1856. Recently, several hundred had been purchased by the Confederacy, which had not yet been able to get its own armories into quantity production. The Dance Brothers in Texas were starting to make revolvers based upon Colt's patents, and George Todd in Austin had been making a copy of the Colt Navy model even before the war had begun. Other gunmakers throughout the South were turning out guns in small lots, trying to make up for the shortage of armament, but most Confederate soldiers were armed with their own pistols and rifles or those captured from Union soldiers.

When Dixon had refused to allow him to handle the LeMatt, Thurlow had felt the man did not want him to know too much about it, and he had pretended total ignorance. But he had seen and handled the revolver several years ago, when the first samples had come to New Orleans from Paris. Of the two barrels, the top one was fitted to fire nine .42-caliber balls, one shot at a time. The center axis on which the cylinder turned was a smoothbore barrel usually loaded with buckshot. The hammer was fitted with a pivot-type striker that allowed it to fire each of the nine percussion loads in the rotating cylinder, while a slight adjustment then allowed the hammer to fall on another percussion cap to fire the smoothbore barrel.

Dixon claimed he had bought the LeMatt from a traveler, but Thurlow suspected he had killed to get it.

The lieutenant settled his hand on the butt of his own revolver. It was a standard 1851 Navy Colt that had been in his family. It had been given to him the day he had enlisted in New Orleans. Thousands of them had been turned out by Samuel Colt to fulfill Yankee military contracts.

Todd Dixon still didn't like the decision and looked down at Thurlow again, scowling. "That's gonna leave us short-handed for any serious fightin'," he offered as a final protest.

"I'm certain you can always recruit some more of Major Quantrill's followers," Thurlow stated cynically, not looking at him. Instead, his eyes were on the four mounds of fresh earth beyond the camels. There really had been no reason to kill the soldiers, but Dixon and his men had shot them down without warning. They had intended to leave the bodies to the buzzards and coyotes, but Thurlow had insisted they be buried. One of them, the sergeant, had been carrying a new woman's wedding ring in a blue plush box. None of the others had liked his order that the ring be buried with the soldier. It would probably have been good for a drink in some desert town saloon.

"We'll rest here today," Thurlow added. "At sundown, we'll move out into the mountains so they can't follow our trail." He glanced at Dixon then, eyes cold in his twenty-three-year-old face. "Is that understood?"

"Yes, sir!" Dixon growled, casting a sloppy salute before he slouched off to join the other half-dozen men. The six of them were all as hard-bitten and slovenly as Dixon, and Lieutenant Russell Wingate Thurlow could not help wondering where Dixon had found them. He was aware they all were killers and the thought already had passed through his mind that ultimately they might kill him. All were roughly dressed, dirty, but not much different than he was himself. He wore a tight-woven Mexican sombrero, sailcloth pants, and a cotton shirt. The desert sun had bronzed his already dark features, helping him to blend with the country and its inhabitants. He knew that, should his true identity become known, he would be shot as a spy.

But they had four camels and that was a start. His plan for getting them past the Yankee patrols and into Texas was simple enough. They were no more than a day's journey from the Mexican border. The two men would drive the camels across the border; then once in Mexico, they would simply head east, following the border until they reached Texas and the Confederate troops who held Fort Davis, where the camel corps was being formed. The fort had been named for Jefferson Davis, when he was Secretary of War for the Union. It was understandable, too, that a fort named for the President of the Confederacy had become one of the first objectives to remove it from Yankee control.

The only problem for the men escorting the camels there could be the Mexican soldiers, but it wasn't likely many would be along the border, while rebellion was fermenting closer to Mexico City.

Intelligence sources said the Yankees already were abandoning the use of camels, even turning some of them out, but those that had been captured at Fort Davis, plus these taken in the ambush, could prove a valuable asset to the Confederate Army in the Southwest.

Nonetheless, as he rested in the shade of the desert tree, Thurlow frowned, wondering just how practical this effort really would prove to be. True, it was Jefferson Davis, as Secretary of War for the United States, who had pushed for importation of the first camel corps of the United States Army. That had been only five years ago, before the strained relationship between North and South had ruptured into open warfare.

Major H.O. Wayne had been put in charge of the experiment and had even gone to Alexandria to buy the first shipment of forty-four camels that had been landed in Texas. Other shipments had come later, but when the first shots had been fired at Fort Sumter, Wayne had resigned his commission and had ridden south. Commissioned in the Army of the Confederate States of America, he had been placed in charge of the Confederacy's effort to start its own camel corps.

Most of the camels imported by the Union Army before the war had been the one-hump variety, chosen for their superior speed as well as strength. As recently as 1857, a train of troopers, with camels and mules, had left Cape Verde on the Texas Coast for a 950-mile trek to Fort Defiance in New Mexico. Reaching this initial goal in record time, the young Navy lieutenant, Edward Beale, leading the strange expedition, had pushed onward to California.

When Beale had returned from his three-thousand-mile trek, he had been filled with tales of the superiority of camels in a desert environment. They needed little water—in fact, had been used to carry kegs from which to water the accompanying mules and the troopers—and they seemed to thrive on sagebrush, manzanita, and even cactus.

Thurlow had learned in his briefings by Major Wayne that the experiment had not been without problems, however. Horses and cattle would flee at sight of the camels and most of the Army handlers hated them. Only the handful of Arabs brought to Texas with the beasts by the Yankee Army had truly understood them, but as the war had become a reality and the Union had started to abandon the experiment, the Arab camel drivers had slowly drifted away.

Many times since he had been given the assignment to procure camels for his army, Lieutenant Thurlow had secretely wondered whether so much importance would have been placed on his mission had not Jefferson Davis been made President of the Confederacy.

It was an odd set of circumstances that had brought him from a Louisiana plantation to the middle of the Mojave Desert. His orders had stated that Dixon could be located in Tucson and would be of help. But when he had found the man in a Mexican brothel, he had not realized his first recruit was a cold blooded killer. Grimly, squinting his eyes now against the sun that made the distant sand dunes dance in the heat, the young officer stared toward the graves where the Yankee sergeant and his men lay buried.

He was authorized to pay Dixon and his gang two hundred and fifty dollars for every camel that arrived at Fort Davis. That seemed a big bunch of money when compared to what soldiers were getting for risking their lives on the battlefield. But he knew that Dixon was expecting more; he just didn't know what.

Chapter Two

It stood to reason that I was a camel jockey because I was low enough in rank that I didn't have nothing to say as to how or where I was used. Even after I earned my corporal's stripes, the Army still ran my life. For beans, hardtack, and a few dollars a month, I was supposed to follow orders without question, and one of those orders had been to report to the camel contingent at Fort Mojave.

I'd been at it for six months now, wondering if I was ever going to quit looking over my shoulder for Apaches and get back East where the real war was going on. I'd enlisted to fight Rebs, not to dodge Indians and play nursemaid for a misfit out of *The Arabian Nights*.

I couldn't understand why Sam Slagle seemed content to be a camel drover. He pretended often enough that he didn't like it, but he didn't gripe about it near as much as one might expect. On the other hand, I reckoned it possible he'd seen all the serious fighting he wanted for his own lifetime. Maybe he figured hide-and-seeking Apaches and sweating the blood out through his body pores in the Mojave Desert was better than being lead man in a charge across some Southern cotton field filled with Rebs.

I'd spent a lot of nights beside our campfires with Sam Slagle and I'd come to listen to him, to learn. He'd mentioned once that the whole idea of a camel corps for the Army had come out of the mind of Jefferson Davis, back when he was Secretary of War for the United States of America.

"But the man's a traitor," I'd protested. "Maybe he was settin' us up even back then to look like a bunch of fools."

Hunkered down beside the fire, drinking coffee from his mess cup, the sergeant had looked at me for a long moment as though considering I might be the fool. Then he shook his head.

"Jeff Davis is one of the smartest military men I ever seen. If'n it hadn't been for him an' his Mississippi Rifles, we'd prob'ly a-lost the Battle at Buena Vista. Instead, when the Mex army charged, he was on one side of a vee with his men and the Third Indiana was on the other. When them Mexican riflemen an' lancers come chargin' into that vee, Davis let 'em come within eighty yards before he opened fire. Their bodies was piled up like cordwood an' that charge 'bout broke the back of the whole Mexican army. Took all the sting right out of 'em."

Slagle had paused as though remembering. He had been there, fighting the Mexican War with the Indiana Volunteers. "Cap'n Davis was old Zack Taylor's son-in-law. They hated each other's guts, but when General Taylor got stuck, it was Cap'n Davis an' his Mississippi boys rushed in to save his force." He shook his head. "You don't hafta like them Rebel boys, Wagner, but don't ever consider they ain't smart. And don't think they don't know how to fight. They do."

Over those long weeks of desert sun and dry camps,

I'd learned a piece here, another piece there about Sergeant Slagle. He had come from Ireland like so many others, expecting the streets of America to be paved with gold. Rather than starve to death, he had joined the Indiana Volunteers. After fighting ended in Mexico, he had been signed up in the Indian Battalion that patrolled the Santa Fe Trail. Their mission was to keep it clear of Indians and safe for the traders that brought their supply trains southwest from Missouri into the badlands, ending up in Santa Fe and points south.

Slagle always allowed it had been a boring life except for occasional brushes with Comanches and once in a while, Apaches. That boredom must have been why he come to volunteer for the camel corps. Like most Irishmen I've known, he had a way with all animals. In the beginning, there had been an Arab camel drover more or less in charge, but when he passed several months without being paid, he just disappeared one night. It was said he'd headed for California to hunt gold, not knowing maybe that the peak of the Gold Rush was long since past.

The camels in our command area were used to transport supplies across the desert from Fort Tejon to Fort Mojave, then southward along the Colorado River to Fort Yuma. Some supplies came up the river to the fort from the Gulf of Baja California, but it was a long trip and not always safe. When the river was low, the vessels couldn't come that far north, so our camels had come to be all the more important. Leastwise, that's what we was told when we'd start growling about camel duty.

Myself, I wasn't so certain our caravan was so all-fired important as they'd have us believe. The wagon route across the desert from San Bernardino had been cut by settlers who come West in '49 for gold. It stood to reason a wagon train could transport a lot more goods to Fort Beale, an outpost we'd passed through twenty-five miles back, and Fort Mojave itself, than we could carry on all the camels of both the Union and the Confederacy.

But I wasn't paid to think, let alone express my views. There was talk that Southern sympathizers were using the old trail to leave California and journey East to join up with the Rebels. A wagon train would be easy prey for them, but it made sense to me that our camel caravan would be even easier to cancel out of the war. Maybe the theory was that a wagon train would be worth plundering, while a few camel loads of supplies wouldn't matter much one way or the other. Of course, there's lots of matters a corporal don't think about out loud, but it had occurred to me that some general back in Washington was trying to build hisself a reputation on our sweat and miseries.

As we rode over the last of the sand dunes and looked across the Colorado to Fort Mojave, I was dreaming of a bath to get the sun stink off my body, and I knew Sam Slagle was thinking in terms of the whiskey at the sutler's store.

Officially, we were attached to the cavalry unit at Fort Mojave, but even when on our home ground, it wasn't like being part of a unit. We were outcasts if ever there was such. The captain in charge wouldn't allow our camels inside the gate of the fort, because they tended to frighten the horses and the cavalry soldiers didn't like them. I figured that dislike was mostly out of fear, since a camel can be a mean, cantankerous beast.

Instead of putting up inside the fort, there was what was known as "the camel camp", set up a couple of hundred yards off to a side of the gate. We had our own picket line, and forage for the beasts was stacked there. We were in the habit of going into the fort for business and pleasure, but we camped outside with our animals at night to be certain one of the cavalrymen didn't turn them all loose and drive them off into the desert. It had been learned the hard way that a camel can travel a lot faster in them desert sands than anyone trying to chase him.

Sam Slagle pulled up Big Red, the camel he always rode, atop that sand dune, and we sat looking down on the fort. There was a town of sorts starting to form around it and there was one new building had gone up since the last time we'd come this way. A stagecoach line had started crossing the desert, too, following one of the old immigrant trails, and the coach was pulled up in front of one of the buildings.

"Gettin' to be a real metropolis, ain't it?" Slagle's Irish brogue came through his words. "Next thing yuh know, they'll want us to dress formal for chow."

I glanced back at the other four camel drovers, who had halted their beasts behind us. They were fidgeting in the strange Arab saddles, wanting Slagle to lead them in so they could tend the beasts and get into the fort or the coming town for food, drink, and maybe that near-dry bath.

Slagle's big red camel was the only one that wasn't loaded down with the supplies we'd hauled in from Fort Tejon. It was our month for that section of the haul, and it wasn't nearly so bad as the stretch from Mojave to Yuma. Every other month, we'd switch and it was another week before we were due to take over the Yuma haul.

Part of our journey had been through the mountains before we had come down into the desert, the heat rising up to meet us. I'd come to think that gradual change from a cool mountaintop to the heat of the desert floor was worse than feeling that same heat all the time. It tended to give you a feeling of dread, as you felt your skin dry out and your thirst grow. But to the camels, it didn't seem to matter. Their pace never changed.

My camel and the others behind me were loaded down with bales and boxes, all lashed to packsaddles copied from those used by the Arabs. We sort of perched on top of that heap, not adding all that much more to the load of near half a ton that each of the camels carried day after day without seeming to notice. Earlier, I'd been told, the camels had been accompanied by cavalry patrols and had been riderless. It hadn't taken long to figure out, though, that the weight of kegged water for both men and horses added more to the loads than just letting a drover ride atop the freight.

Looking back, I could see that Sid Jordan was wearying and needing some rest. He had a big Colt .44 Dragoon revolver strapped to his saddle like the rest of us, since it was too heavy to carry on a belt all the time. Balanced in front of him was an official Army issue Model 1855 rifled carbine. It had a short barrel and fired a .56-caliber slug that would knock down a bull buffalo without him ever offering a kick. It was the same carbine that armed the rest of us, except for the sergeant. Across his saddle, Slagle carried a .44 Colt revolving carbine. While our carbines were single-shot and had to be reloaded from the muzzle after every shot, his was loaded in the cylinder just like that of the Third Model Dragoons we'd all been issued. He said the army had issued him the Colt carbine when he was with the Indian Battalion, but there were no government markings or proofs on it. I'd sort of figured he bought it with his own money.

One thing he favored about the Colt carbine, besides the fact that the cylinder held five bullets, was the fact that it fired the same size slug as his Dragoon. He'd griped long and often about Army brass that couldn't understand how a rifle and a revolver should fire the same load. Realizing that I could never interchange the bullets between my own Dragoon and carbine, if one of them quit on me in a bad spot, I'd come to sympathize mightily with Slagle's views.

"They ever get that railroad built cross country they're talkin' about, all this is gonna change," the sergeant said thoughtfully. "Prob'ly not for the better. Easy transportation brings strange folks into a place."

"I don't reckon we'll be around to see that happen." I was anxious as the others to get down to what passed for civilization.

It was near dark when we crossed the river ford and rode into the camp. It was deserted, and even in the twilight gloom I could see that no other camels had been held there in recent days. That I thought strange.

I growled a command that was supposed to be Arabic to the camel I rode and it slowly got down on its knees so I could slide to the ground without too much of a drop. I stood there, weary and stiff, thinking maybe being shot at by them Rebs back East might have its advantages. Slagle gave a command, but the red camel ignored him, moving toward the stack of fodder that edged the arena.

"Hold up, you slab-sided son of Satan!" Slagle shouted at him, jerking on the crude rope halter. "Get down on your knees before I climb offa here an' shoot you through your fool head!"

He turned the red camel in a circle and after a moment, the beast stopped and slowly knelt, while Slagle slid down its side, pausing to beat the dust from his heavy uniform shirt. He looked up as a horseman came through the gates of the fort and trotted the several hundred yards to where we waited. Behind us, there were more curses as the other drovers got down from their animals.

"You're to report to Captain Wright, Sergeant," the horseman announced, disdainfully wheeling his horse in a circle to show his superiority. He glanced at me. "You, too, Corporal."

Slagle spat into the dust and glared at the cavalry private. "Get that damned horse outa here before one of my camels eats 'im. Maybe you, too."

The horseman offered an airy wave of his hand and set his blunt spurs in the horse's flanks to gallop back to the post. Slagle turned to our other four drovers.

"Get them packs off the beasts and get 'em settled in." Already a heavy wagon was coming out the gate, headed toward us. One man on foot was carrying a coal oil lantern, but what surprised me was that a detail of four soldiers marched behind the wagon, their rifles at shoulder arms position. I could see by Slagle's frown that he had seen the armed guard, too, and didn't understand. It was normal for the quartermaster to sort out the gear we had brought, segregating the supplies that would stay here from those that would be sent on to Fort Yuma. But this was the first time I had ever seen the wagon under guard.

"Jordan," Slagle ordered, "you'll stand the first watch. Four hours. Simpson, you get cleaned up an' relieve him. Stay sober. That'll give him a chance to wash before he beds down. I'll take the last watch."

Inside the fort, colors long since had been lowered from the wooden flagpole in the center of the compound and troopers strolled about, visiting or headed for the sutler's store, the center of evening social life.

Captain Wright was waiting for us at the door of his headquarters. We saluted and he returned it rather casually, frowning, as he led the way inside. An orderly stood at attention, but Wright ignored him as he led us into his office and closed the door. He moved behind his desk and sat down, while we both came to attention and waited. It was important, if he wanted to talk without a chance for us to clean the dust off. Good officers take consideration for their men and animals and I'd come to consider Captain Wright as that kind.

"Stand at ease." He stared at Slagle. "From the words

of endearment I heard clear from the camel camp, you still have no great use for camels, Sergeant."

Slagle, standing at ease now, glanced down at the officer. "No, sir. An' since I've done my time in hell with them beasts, I'm wonderin' how soon I kin get back with the horse cavalry."

"You might not like camels, Sergeant, but you're the only man on this post who can handle them with any major degree of success. You might say you're our camel expert."

"It's more a case of that red devil likin' the taste of my hide," Slagle muttered. It was a sort of play-acting exchange they went through on a regular basis.

The captain motioned to the chairs in front of his desk. "Sit down. Both of you."

I was a little self-conscious about sitting down in the presence of an officer right in his own office, but Slagle flopped into the chair like he was going to take a lease on it and needed to try it for size and comfort. The captain fidgeted with some papers, frowning at them for several seconds before he looked up.

"As you both know, when the war started, we had a sizeable camel detachment in Texas. The Rebels have captured the fort there and are now using our animals. According to intelligence reports, the Confederate Army plans on building their camel corps into a major transportation link. For that, they need camels and they need money."

He stared at us for a moment as though to see whether we were listening. Then he added, "The war's catching up to us."

Neither Sergeant Slagle nor I knew what he meant, and it must have showed in our faces.

"A patrol found Sergeant Tuppy and his men this afternoon," Wright went on slowly. "They'd been ambushed and their camels driven south toward the border."

"Sounds like Apaches, sir," I suggested. Them Indians had come to know our soldiers weren't allowed to cross the border. They'd often launch raids across the line, then hurry back into Mexican territory where they couldn't be followed. But Captain Wright shook his head.

"Not likely. The tracks showed their horses were all shod. And Tuppy and each of his men was buried in a neat grave. No Apache ever did that."

"Sounds like organization," Slagle said slowly. "No band of renegades would hang about for a buryin' either."

"It sounds like Confederates," the captain agreed. "That's why I sent for both of you."

I'd been wondering about that ever since the messenger had said the officer wanted both of us. Usually, it was Slagle alone who reported to the fort commander.

"Tuppy's camels are across the border by now. Gone. You're going to have to take the supplies on to Fort Yuma." Wright offered a wry smile that didn't offer much comfort. "As far as they've come, another two hundred miles or so shouldn't make that much difference."

He was right about that. Most of those supplies, instead of coming overland from the East, either came from California itself or around the Horn by merchant ship. Landed in San Diego or Los Angeles, they were moved to Fort Tejon and other outposts at the edge of the desert by wagon, then transferred to the camels.

"As I said, the Confederacy needs money badly, Sergeant, and even the financial credit of the Union doesn't appear all that good at this moment."

He was riddling us again and both the sergeant and myself had our eyes on him, wondering.

"Some of the suppliers around Fort Yuma, especially those furnishing beef and horses to the Army, are beginning to doubt the value of our paper money. They want gold."

Slagle shook his head. "That stands to reason, Captain, but that couldn't be why Dan Tuppy was killed. He was comin' away from Yuma."

"He was killed for his camels. I have no doubt of that," the officer said. "Actually, whoever ambushed him was too early. Had they hit his outfit on the way back to Yuma, they would have scored big." He hesitated, concentrating his stare on me long enough to make me feel discomfort. I hadn't had my corporal's stripes so long that I felt fully secure about them staying sewed to my tunic.

"Corporal Wagner, I asked you in with Sergeant Slagle for one reason. Should the sergeant be killed, you would be in command of the camel train. Understood?"

"Yes, sir." That much made sense. That's the way the military has always worked. The next in command takes over.

"That's why both of you must know exactly what's going on." He hesitated, maybe wondering whether I really should be in the room. Then he plunged on. "Do you remember that keg of nails you brought in with the supplies?"

In that moment, the four-man guard detail following the quartermaster wagon started to make sense. I even knew what he was going to say next.

"There's ten thousand dollars in gold coin from the San Francisco mint in that keg. You will get it to Yuma!"

Chapter Three

I reckon I should've felt honored, if that's the right word, when Captain Wright stood me up there beside Sergeant Slagle to tell me the hard facts of what already had come about and what we likely would face before we got that gold to Yuma. But I didn't thank the man for his confidence. I knew more of the happenings and circumstance than a corporal ought to, and I found that knowledge fearsome.

"You'll be a sergeant soon enough, if this war lasts any time at all." Slagle was leaning against the crude bar. "And like the captain said, anything happens to me, you hafta know where you stand."

"Then let's make damned sure nothin' happens to you," I said, more positive than maybe I felt. "I don't like the thought of bein' out there with a buncha renegades, Apaches or whatever."

Slagle shook his head, after taking a pull at his bottle. "It wasn't neither. It was soldiers."

I found it hard to believe. "A soldier'd just shoot down four men like that?"

"A soldier'd see they got buried proper. A renegade

woulda just left them to the buzzards. An Injun'd strip their clothes an' anything else, then leave 'em. It was Rebel soldiers."

Sam Slagle had told me once that "most Irishmen can't drink, they just think they can." There were times when he was hell-bent on proving he was the exception; all too often, he became the proof. I cast him a quick look now, taking in the level of the bottle in that glance. He had put a hole in the contents, but he wasn't drunk. He'd volunteered himself for the late watch and I knew him well enough to figure he'd be sober for that. He wouldn't stand for one of his men being drunk on guard and he was the sort to set the example. He'd told me enough times that setting the example was mostly what soldiering was all about, whether on the parade ground or in battle.

Captain Wright had told us a lot of other things, too. The Piutes to the north of us had been kicking up a fuss, one more reason wagon trains didn't venture into the Mojave Desert. Down south were the Mojaves and the Yumas. The former were pretty harmless, but the Yumas tended to be sneaky and wanted a man well outnumbered before they'd move to turn him into buzzard bait. The real trouble was the Apaches. They held out mostly in the Arizona Territory, but in recent months, they'd been coming farther and farther West on their raids.

The fact that folks around Yuma were set on being paid off in gold for supplies and services didn't have to do with Indians, though. It was the Confederates. According to Captain Wright, not only were Southern sympathizers moving eastward out of California, trying to get to Texas, but there was a big Confederate force—some of them just secessionists without uniforms to be sure—forming near Tucson. It was talked that they planned to surround Fort Tucson and starve out the Union garrison.

Captain Wright was handling things in a way I'm not

certain was how I'd have done it. But I reckoned I wasn't ever likely to be a captain, so it was the sort of decision I wasn't ever likely to worry over.

When Sergeant Tuppy's outfit had been a day late on the trail from Yuma, some two hundred miles to the south on the Colorado, the captain had sent out a mounted patrol to look for him. They'd found the graves and had come back to report. What with the gold shipment we'd brought in from San Bernardino, he said he didn't want a lot of talk around his fort, so he had sent the whole horse troop west to Fort Beale to scout out of there for a day or two while he had a chance to sort things out.

Thinking back, I'd not noticed any extra cavalry troops at Beale when we'd slogged through there, stopping only long enough to water, but it could have been the troop was out scouting the country. Fort Beale was named for the Navy officer who had made the first trip from Texas to California with the camels. It wasn't much as a fort, but then neither was Fort Mojave. Yuma was the largest in the area, since it was the supply base for all of the forts and camps along the Colorado River and even those far out in the desert.

Fort Yuma was in the state of California, while right across the river, Arizona City was in Arizona Territory. You couldn't look across the Colorado to that wide-open town without being discouraged by the sight of the old adobe-built Territorial Prison. It was said to be a real hell hole where few men ever escaped. If a prisoner did escape, the custom was to put a price on his head and send the Yaqui scouts out to collect it. More often than not, they'd come back days later with the poor feller's head in a blood-soaked sack. The Indian scouts would be paid off and would sit around waiting—maybe even hoping—for another escape. Sometimes, though, they'd come back with Apache heads. The only good thing about a Yaqui, some said, was that he didn't like Apaches.

I'd asked Slagle once about this bounty system and he'd told me how it had been a dozen years back, when the Army in New Mexico and Arizona had put a price on Apaches. Right off, several firms were formed for the express purpose of hiring bounty hunters to collect Apache scalps and sell them to the Army. It didn't matter whether that hair came from men, women, or children, old or the young, so long as they were Apaches.

"You can't hardly expect an Apache to feel kindly toward us white-eyes and 'specially the Army," Slagle had said. I'd spent days wondering if he was just trying to get under my skin with a pack of tales, but I'd learned later that what he said was true.

The sutler had one room at the back of his store that was set up as a bar for the fort's soldiers. It wasn't much, just a barren place lit by coal oil lamps with some rough planks stretched across a couple of barrels to serve as a bar.

Old Snead, the sutler, knew he was in business at the pleasure of the United States Army and that, if things got radical in his place, he could be put out of the sutler business in a hurry. So he tended to be careful how much liquor he sold any one trooper. If it looked like there was going to be a fight, he'd just close up and send everybody on their way. If soldiers wanted to fight behind the stables, that was not his affair. Or if one wanted to buy a bottle and go sit on the riverbank to get stink-eyed drunk, that wasn't his business either.

He tended to keep a wary eye on certain of his customers, and this night Old Snead was watching Slagle, gauging how much he drank. Sam had torn the place up once and Snead didn't favor a repetition. I couldn't figure why he was so tense this night, until I heard someone say it had been payday. That meant there would be more than the usual drinking, singing, and laughing. All of them pleasures could blend into a sudden fight. I'd learned that long ago. It started as I was considering the likelihood and wondering how fast I could get out the door.

"Hey, Slagle, you still wet-nursing those four-legged hunchbacks?" a cavalryman demanded loudly. He glanced about, jerking his head toward my sergeant, inviting the others to laugh. There were several chuckles, but not from any who'd seen Sam Slagle fight before.

Slagle didn't tense up at the jibe as one might expect, but Old Snead sure did, knowing trouble clouds when he seen them turning black. Sergeant Slagle sort of turned on the other cavalryman easy-like, smiling.

"Thompson, th' only hunchback I ever knew was your sister, an' she smelled worse than any camel!"

"I don't have a sister," Thompson said, grinning back. His own bottle was on one of the plank tables and the level made it plain he was well into it.

"But I've got a camel," Slagle answered. That was when he swung.

The cavalryman may have expected the fist, but it didn't make much difference. It caught him on the point of the chin and his head snapped back. His body kept going in the same direction till he hit the floor and skidded into a table. Other soldiers were sitting there, sipping the warm beer Old Snead slopped together from river water, hops, and yeast. They yelled as foam sloshed out of their mugs, but none got up to face Slagle. He was still at the bar, seeming all relaxed and unconcerned.

Thompson sat up, daze-eyed, not certain just where he was. Slagle walked over, hauled him to his feet, and, with a sudden twist, had his arm up behind his back.

"It's time you got to know what lovin' creatures them camels really are," the sergeant declared quietly, marching Thompson toward the door. The cavalryman knew right then what Slagle was about, for he twisted about and swore something fierce. But Sam just tightened the hold on his arm, shoving it up between his shoulder blades till Thompson brayed with hurt.

Some of the others started to follow, but Slagle half turned with a baleful sort of look. "This don't concern none of you." Then he glanced at me. "Get the door."

I shoved the door open and stepped aside so he could shove Thompson through. I didn't know whether his comment included me, but I didn't see no future as the only camel drover alone with a squadron of horse soldiers. I wasn't far behind as he quick-marched Thompson across the parade ground to the small door in the stockade wall near the big gate.

"Let us through," Slagle ordered the sentry. "This man's sick. We gotta get him to the camel camp."

Thompson tried to say something, but Slagle pushed that twisted arm up another notch which tended to make him silent right sudden. The soldier on guard hesitated, then unbolted the log door and shoved it open. After we was through, I glanced back. The sentry seemed uncertain about what he should do, but he solved the problem by shutting the door. I heard the heavy bolt as it was shoved home.

"Slagle, I'll kill you!" Thompson threatened, as my sergeant propelled him across the uneven ground.

"Better people've tried," Slagle said cheerfully.

"Who's there?" Sid Jordan challenged out of the near darkness. One coal oil lamp was burning at the edge of the encampment and I could make him out, outlined as he was in its yellow light.

"Sergeant Slagle an' Corporal Wagner," was the reply. "With a friend."

Slagle shoved Thompson past Jordan and full up

against Big Red. The camel was munching hay, but turned its head to cast an unhappy eye at the cavalryman. Maybe he smelled horse odor on the man. Whatever it was, he didn't like it.

"This is Big Red," Slagle announced, swinging the horse soldier so he was face to face with the beast. "Kiss him an' you'll come to love 'im!"

"Dammit, Sam!" The horse soldier wriggled under the hold.

"Kiss him!" Slagle shoved him forward until Thompson's face was buried in the camel's cheek. I thought Big Red might try to bite his face off, but the beast just stood there as though accepting he was part of the fun. Slagle jerked Thompson back, allowing him to breathe.

"See?" Slagle's tone was soothing, almost friendly. "Camels ain't so bad. 'Nother treatment or so, you'll be full in love."

"I'll kill you!" Thompson's threat was little more than a groan through his pain.

"Not tonight, bucko." Slagle whirled him about and turned him loose. That was when Big Red, still chewing, chose to show one of his nastier tricks. He belched heavy-like, then spit the half-masticated hay full into Thompson's face. The cavalry soldier stood there, brown, tobacco-like drizzle rolling down his face.

"You sonuvagun!" he snarled. But instead of trying Slagle again, he lurched off into the night.

Slagle, suddenly a sergeant again, turned on Sid Jordan. "Where's Simpson? Time he relieved you."

"I'm here." The other camel drover came out of the blackness, grinning at what he'd witnessed. There was no formality in the changing of the guard. Jordan simply handed Simpson the carbine and made for the lamplight.

"I s'pose you fixed it so's I can't go get a drink an' be

safe." Jordan's tone was a cross between bitterness and amusement.

"I don't think I'd go in there by myself, at least," the sergeant agreed.

"There ain't much else to do but bed down." Jordan turned to the pile of loose hay where he had spread his blankets.

"Won't hurt any of us to get some rest." Slagle settled on a packsaddle, pulling off his boots. "We're movin' out at dawn."

"Where?" Jordan demanded, surprised. We rated two days' rest before starting back to Fort Tejon.

"Yuma." The sergeant glanced at me. "And don't ask questions."

"I want to go with you, Sergeant."

The voice surprised us all. Simpson leveled the carbine before the girl came into the circle of light thrown off by our lantern. I couldn't see her well, but she was young, her dark hair piled on top of her head like I'd seen in fashion drawings, and she wore one of them long-skirted traveling outfits.

"Who're you, miss?" Sergeant Slagle was frowning at her. "This ain't no place for you."

"After the display I just saw, I agree, but I'm rather desperate."

"For what?"

"I have to get to Yuma."

Slagle cast a glance in the direction of the town. "You come in on the stage?"

"They have a broken wheel and nobody will say how soon they'll be able to go on." I could see she was pretty, when she came closer to the light. Her nose was maybe a mite long and she was frowning, but she was a lot prettier than the other women in these desert outposts, if they were dumb enough to be there at all. "There's talk of a raid by Apaches. I think the driver's afraid to go on."

Slagle thought about it before he nodded agreement. "If Injuns're spookin' around, the driver's smart."

"That doesn't help me get to Yuma, Sergeant. I'm to be married." She was struck by a sudden thought. "You must know Sergeant Tuppy. He was to meet me here."

Slagle seen me jerk at mention of the name. He gave me a little shake of his head, frowning a warning.

"Sergeant Tuppy went to Yuma." It wasn't really a lie. Dan Tuppy had gone to Yuma. The rest of what Slagle said wasn't a lie neither. "He ain't comin' back here."

"I heard you say you were leaving at dawn," the girl said. "I have to go with you."

"No you don't." Slagle's tone was rude, unlike the way I'd ever heard him talk to any women before. "We ain't runnin' no escort for brides. You'd best wait till that wheel's fixed."

"You don't understand," the girl protested. There was steel in her voice and Slagle recognized it.

"No. I don't understand, but I know how it's gonna be. You ain't goin' with us."

The girl stood there, staring at Slagle, then she sort of swept the rest of us with her dark eyes, like she was seeking a vote. I looked away, sort of embarrassed for her.

"Then I'll have to find another way." She turned back into the dark.

"Yes, ma'am," Slagle called after her. "Wait for that stage."

We just stood staring at the blackness where she had disappeared into the night. Finally, I looked at Slagle. "She seems determined."

"Yeah, but why?" he asked shortly. "This country's

alive with secessionists. Maybe she already knows Dan Tuppy's dead."

And I thought again of the innocent-looking nail keg that had been taken away under guard. It would be brought back at dawn and strapped onto one of the camels.

"You think she's a spy?" I was half whispering, but Jordan and Simpson must have heard.

"Dan Tuppy was a fool for the ladies," Slagle said. "An' she's enough to make one lose caution."

Chapter Four

The strange rider came into the mountain camp before dawn, his horse nearly spent. Thurlow, awakened by his arrival, saw that Todd Dixon was fully clothed, sitting beside the protected fire. The Confederate officer watched from his blankets, while Dixon and this new arrival hunkered beside the low blaze, talking in low tones. The rider chewed at a handful of jerky Dixon had shoved at him, talking between mouthfuls. But they were far enough away and talking in such low tones that the officer was unable to hear what was said.

Thurlow realized the man was a messenger and had brought news of some kind to Dixon. The renegade leader rose to pace the clearing, considering, scowling. Once in a while, he paused to squat beside the rider, asking more questions, scowling over the answer he got. Several times he glanced in Thurlow's direction, but the lieutenant feigned sleep.

It was still dark when Dixon began to move about the circle of sleeping men, toeing them awake, talking to each of them in low tones. The others already were folding their blankets, pulling on their boots, when Dixon bent over Thurlow, shaking his shoulder.

"Yes? What is it?" Thurlow sat up slowly, pretending confusion and rubbing his eyes as though just awakening.

"We'll be movin' out, Lootenant," Dixon growled. "Chance to take some more camels maybe."

Thurlow glanced from him to the man at the fire. The stranger was pouring coffee from a smoke-blackened pot into a tin cup. "Who's he?"

"He just rode in. He says there'll be another camel train headed for Yuma today or tomorrow." Dixon glanced toward the exhausted rider. "He came from Fort Tejon, where he's been watchin' things. He stopped in Fort Mojave long enough to get the lay of what's happenin'."

"What's he say?"

"The Yankees found them dead camel troopers. Sent out a patrol when they didn't turn up on time."

Thurlow had thrown back the saddle blanket in which he had dozed, full sleep coming. There, high up in the Chocolate Mountains, it had been cold after midnight and he had felt the chill biting through the layer of wool even before the messenger had ridden in. He was not used to such temperatures in his native Louisiana and had wondered how the others withstood the discomfort so well.

"Are they following us?" Thurlow wanted to know, glancing into the darkness of the valley below. It was just more desert, which had been one of the reasons for selecting the spot for their camp. They could see anyone coming miles away.

"Reckon not," Todd Dixon replied, shaking his head. "In fact there's somethin' strange 'bout what's goin' on."

Thurlow waited and Dixon continued. "The patrol reported back to Fort Mojave, then the whole outfit was sent to Fort Beale to look for Injun sign." He paused, giving his words some thought, mulling the possibilities.

"It's like that captain in charge wanted them men outta the way. Didn't want no talk. Talk at Mojave says the patrol was took by Apaches."

"You believe that's what they really think?" Thurlow's soft New Orleans drawl was hardened by his concern. He could see his mission becoming suddenly more complicated.

"Don't know," Dixon replied. "We'd best see what's goin' on."

The others already were saddling their horses. The officer looked at Todd Dixon, then glanced to where his own bay was picketed. "Better have someone saddle my horse."

"This ain't like no spit-an-shine Army post, Lootenant," the renegade replied coldy. "We all do for our own selves."

Thurlow, still seated, had been reaching for his boots, but he looked up then at Dixon. It was the first instance of outright disobedience. He stared into the other man's slitted eyes, seeing the yellow animal-like glint by the low light from the fire. He hadn't expected open rebellion so soon. Gritting his teeth, he pulled on his boots and rose, as Dixon turned away, making for his own horse.

Dixon claimed to have served with Quantrill's raiders in guerrilla attacks upon the anti-slavery Kansas Jayhawkers that had gone on even before the war had broken out, but the young Confederate had his doubts. There was a south Texas twang in the other man's voice. Quantrill's men were almost all Missourians. Dixon may have fled Texas to avoid ending up in the uniform of the Confederacy, but if that was so, why had Thurlow been told to contact Dixon in Tucson? He shook his head as he picked up the battered Spanish saddle and the blankets in which he had tried to sleep.

The sun was well up when Dixon raised his hand in

signal and the rest of the motley band of riders drew rein behind him. Thurlow, riding at his elbow, was surprised at the sudden signal.

"What's the matter, Dixon?" he asked. Back in Louisiana or Texas, he would have called the man by his rank, but in spite of the fact that Dixon insisted he was a sergeant for Quantrill, Thurlow felt an odd reluctance to address him by military title. It was a reaction he was unable to explain even to himself beyond the vague feelings that the use of the rank with Todd Dixon would degrade it.

He looked down the steep hillside in the same direction that Dixon was staring and recognized the terrain. This was the site where the massacre of the camel caravan had taken place three days ago. But it had changed. The graves he had ordered dug and covered now were hastily opened holes, unorderly heaps of sand around them. The area was crossed and recrossed by hoof prints as though a mounted patrol had been there for hours.

"Well, they know it wasn't Injuns," Dixon declared thoughtfully, folding both hands across his saddlehorn and staring down at the empty scene. "They dug up the bodies an' hauled 'em back to the fort. No Injun ever buries anyone he kills. They'd know that. We shoulda scalped 'em an' left 'em lay."

Thurlow realized Dixon was blaming him for his own insistence that the dead soldiers be treated as something other than carrion. Slowly, he turned in his saddle to look at the rest of the band bunched behind them. Dirty, surly, and ill-clothed, they had already shown they were an unprincipled lot and that it took a strong hand to control them. Dixon obviously had that control.

But in looking them over, the officer could not help but think of his own grandfather. Turning back to survey the endless stretch of Mojave sand, he remembered Padras Island off the south Texas coast. The rolling sands of the desert were much like those of that tiny coastal island that he remembered as being devoid of vegetation, except for the scattered growth of palmetto.

He had gone there with his grandfather supposedly to fish when he was twelve, but they had remained only a day. When they had returned to New Orleans by boat from Corpus Christi, the gnarled old man had carried a strange-looking chest in his arms. He had not allowed it to be stored with the baggage during the short voyage, never letting it out of his sight. It had not been until after the death of his grandfather, Jules Dupree, that Thurlow had learned the old man had once been a pirate and had sailed with Jean Lafitte to terrorize the Caribbean.

Following the old man's funeral ten years ago, his mother had taken him aside to explain that the money to buy their plantation had been brought by old Dupree from the tiny Texas island in that iron-bound chest. It had been some of the loot that Lafitte and his pirates had buried decades before. The only others who had known its actual whereabouts had been killed in the War of 1812, when the pirates led by Lafitte had joined with Andrew Jackson to fight against the British and save New Orleans from the torch.

After the battle, Lafitte had sailed away to disappear. But Jules Dupree had stayed in New Orleans, where he had married and become a slave trader. The wealthy plantation, bought with slave money and pirate treasure, had passed to Thurlow's mother when the old pirate had died.

Russell Thurlow remembered his grandfather as a kindly but bumbling old man, more interested in cultivating roses than in knowing what went on in the world. It was as though he had tried to shut out reality in his last years, shielding his conscience against his deeds committed as a pirate and against the misery he had created in the slave trade.

Surveying Todd Dixon's motley renegades, the officer could not help wondering whether his Grandfather Dupree had once been like them. They too were pirates of a sort, all of them. They rode horses rather than ships, but pillage and murder were their way of life, their livelihood. Still, he couldn't imagine any of them living to become old men who tended roses.

"You think they'll quit sending the camels?" Thurlow demanded.

Dixon considered the question, his expression sullen and moody. Finally he shook his head. "No. They gotta move them supplies. An' prob'ly the gold, too."

"Gold?" Thurlow couldn't hide his surprise. Dixon turned to look at him, yellowed teeth showing in a wolfish grin.

"Might be my spies're better'n yourn, Lootenant." Dixon jerked his head to indicate their back trail. "Simm's been watchin' at Fort Tejon for a coupla weeks." The lone messenger had been left back in the mountain encampment, his jaded horse too far gone to join the others. "He says a shipment of gold was brought in there in a wagon, then it just sorta disappeared. I figger it was sent on to Fort Mojave on them camels. From there, it's gotta get to Yuma."

Thurlow, frowning, was not certain exactly what he was being told, but it was obvious Dixon was enjoying his seeming superiority to trained military leadership.

"We got some people in Arizona Territory's spent a lotta time convincin' folks the Yankees' paper money ain't no good, that they oughtta get paid in gold for the cows 'n' horses 'n' other stuff the cavalry buys from 'em. Looks like the effort's gonna pay off."

"They'll try to move gold by camel train?" Thurlow recognized his own doubt in his tone. The animals, slow moving, would stand little chance against a band of armed horseman. That had been proven three days ago.

"How else they gonna get it to Yuma? The river's too low to send it by boat." Dixon shook his head, offering a grimace of disgust. "We shoulda let that first caravan go through. They'll be lookin' for trouble now."

"They'll have an armed escort," Thurlow observed. "That could make it difficult."

"Could be. We'll just hafta wait 'n' see." Dixon looked toward the line of sand dunes several miles away. Beyond them, Thurlow knew, wound the Colorado River. The accepted trail between Fort Mojave and Fort Yuma generally parallelled the course of the river. However, observation over a two-week period had shown that the caravans usually stayed several miles away from the stream. Thus, they avoided the clouds of mosquitoes and other biting insects that inhabited the lowlands flanking the water. At sundown, it had been noted, the camel drovers usually moved to the river to allow the camels to drink and to fill their own canteens, then the caravans would move back into the desert, away from the insects and the fevers that were a danger, if one stayed too close to the river for any length of time. Night camps always were a couple of miles from the banks of the river.

Thurlow nodded to indicate the now-empty graves and the signs of horse traffic below. "This place is no good. They'll expect us to hit them here."

"We're agreein' on that," Dixon growled, squinting his eyes against the sun that already was baking their skins, causing even the hardened horses to sweat. "We'll find another likely spot downstream. After they pass here an' ain't been attacked, they'll maybe get careless."

"How much gold do you think they have? Or didn't your spy tell you that?"

Dixon cast those yellow eyes upon him once more,

judging, then shook his head, forcing the wolfish grin. "Figgers to be sufficient. Takes a batch of money to run a cavalry post. Besides, Yuma's the big supply depot for this whole desert."

"The Confederacy can use that gold." Thurlow was watching the renegade's face. He did not miss the shadow that passed behind Dixon's eyes even as he grinned and nodded agreement.

"That's right, Lootenant." The man's tone was smooth with assurances. "The South needs money for guns 'n' horses a lot more'n them Yankees do."

In that moment, Lieutenant Russell Wingate Thurlow knew he probably was going to die and that the Confederacy never would see the Yankee gold, if it really existed.

Chapter Five

"Sergeant, we're bein' follered!"

Able Smith said it softly, as he rode his camel up beside Sam Slagle and pulled the beast in. Slagle squinted beneath the brim of his government-issue felt hat, staring back along our route. I looked, too, but all I seen was the stretch of near-white sand that dazzled the eyes. No sign of movement.

"How many?" Slagle wanted to know, still staring.

"Dunno." Corporal Smith shook his head. "Only seen one rider."

Slagle glanced at him, offering a funny sort of grin. "That means we're surrounded. They's another one ahead of us. He rode outta Mojave a coupla hours ahead of us durin' my watch."

"Who was it?" I wanted to know. Slagle just shook his head.

"Someone from town. He didn't come around for introductions."

For being the second in command of the caravan, there was a mighty lot I wasn't being told. It hadn't taken long to figure that out even before daylight.

Slagle, ending his watch, had rolled us out long before reveille and seen that we got fed in the fort mess before he put us all to loading camels, tying down the bunglesome packs. The wagon had been driven out from the fort with that keg marked as nails, as well as some other supply goods, and Slagle had me help lash the keg to my own saddle where I'd have a continuing watch on it. Neither of us treated it like it was anything but iron nails, but I wondered if any of the others suspected. Able Smith did appear sort of surprised that it took a sergeant and another corporal to lash down a keg of nails, but he said nothing.

I knew Smith only slightly and I'd been right confused when him and his men rode into our camp only a short time after Slagle had sent that woman off into the night with her anger. Smith's outfit worked out of Fort Beale, usually supplying outposts to the north, and I figured at first maybe they'd come to Mojave to relieve us and make the regular trip back to Fort Tejon.

But I found that wasn't the way it wasn't to be at all. They was joining up with us to haul south to the supply depot at Fort Yuma. Leastwise, that was the line Slagle was putting out, but I couldn't help but wonder if the real reason wasn't to give us added strength and more guns should we run into the kind of trouble Dan Tuppy's outfit had met up with.

Smith's drovers had offloaded their camels, tossed some hay to them, then the corporal and his four men had settled down to get as much sleep as they could before we started south.

"You know what this is all about?" I asked Smith the next morning, after Slagle had gone to the fort for a final word with Captain Wright.

Able had shook his head at me. "I don't know nothin' at all, 'cept we scraped up alla the supplies they could spare at Beale, then they tole us to come down here to join up with Sergeant Slagle an' go on to Yuma with you all." He glanced at the combined strength of the two sections of camels, chewing thoughtfully on a wisp of hay. "They must be gettin' powerful low on supplies downriver or they're gettin' ready for a siege."

I wondered whether he had heard any of the talk about how the Confederates were forming up to surround Fort Tucson and maybe try to starve out the garrison there. Probably that was what it was all about, but I didn't ask.

Smith glanced at the keg of nails now lashed to my camel's saddle. "We've hauled enough damned nails to start an iron mine," he observed. "There's a lot more of them in this country than there's lumber to nail 'em in."

Slagle had been passed through the gate of the fort by the sentry and was moving toward us, almost running. "Get at it!" he shouted. "We're gonna spend a lotta time in the sun!"

He surprised me some more when we'd started out. Usually, we followed the trail down the Arizona side of the river, but this time, mounted on Big Red, he led us back down to Beale's Crossing, where that Navy lieutenant had crossed into California on that first trek with camels. Slagle led us back across the shallows of the Colorado, then moved inland a good three miles before angling southward.

Getting away from the river was something we did near always. It kept us clear from the biting insects and the rattlesnakes that tended to hide from the heat in the low brush that flanked close to both sides of the river.

It didn't take me long to figure out that Slagle, or maybe Captain Wright, had decided on the California side as maybe being safer than the Arizona trail. That was where Dan Tuppy's outfit had been ambushed. If whoever done it was waiting along the Arizona side, we'd be making it a bit harder for them.

But with Able Smith's discovery that we had someone following our tracks, I wondered just how smart we had been. I was bothered a bit, too, by the fact that Sam Slagle didn't seem all that much surprised nor did he seem to feel it unusual that someone had ridden out of Fort Mojave ahead of us by a couple of hours.

"You think the rider from town went to warn someone we're comin'?" I asked. Slagle's reply was a shrug, as he bit into a plug of tobacco.

"No way of tellin'." He was watching our backtrail again. "We'll know soon enough, I reckon."

I eyed the camels strung out behind us. Smith, riding at the tail, had shouted for Slagle to hold up, then had rode forward to report the rider.

"Looks to me like we've put all our camels in one basket," I said.

"I said th' same to Cap'n Wright," Slagle agreed, "but he has somethin' of a plan."

Able Smith'd been around the Army a lot longer than me and probably had rights to think he should have been second to Slagle, but he hadn't indicated any such thought. Nonetheless, he had a reputation for being a knowing soldier and a good one.

"He's set us up as the bait!" Smith accused. "He's gonna foller an', should we get attacked, that'll give him a chance to smash 'em?"

"Somethin' like that," Slagle agreed, still squinting to the rear. I seen the rider at the same time he did, nothing more than a large black speck topping the crest of a sand dune. He followed our tracks until he disappeared behind another hill of sand.

"What're we gonna do 'bout 'im?" Smith wanted to

know. He jerked his chin to indicate the spot where the rider had dropped from sight.

"I'm thinkin' on it." Slagle brushed his shirt sleeve across his face to blot his sweat. It wasn't yet ten o'clock, but what had been a peaceful, even beautiful wasteland at dawn was turning into the type of hell we had all come to hate. It was already a blaster day. "I understan' why there's a rider ahead of us, if he rode out to tell someone we're comin', but why put someone on our backtrail?"

Smith was watching Slagle with a knowing expression. They had soldiered together before. "They's one way to find out."

"There ain't nothin' in my orders to cover this sorta possibility." Slagle was thinking aloud. Then he glanced at Smith and grinned. "Let's do it!"

Able Smith turned to bawl orders at the other drovers. They made for the tops of the dunes, forming a semicircle around the hollow where the three of us still sat our camels. Slagle squinted at the preparations, watching the beasts and their riders disappear over the crests. A few moments later, the soldiers snaked forward on their bellies taking up positions, rifles ready.

"A lot of readyin' for one rider," I said. Slagle ignored me and pointed to a clump of manzanita that stood at the top of one of the dunes.

"We'll take up positions there." He prodded Big Red forward and Smith and I fell our beasts in behind him. On the other side of the dune, we tied the halter ropes to some scrubby brush and crawled back up through the loose sand to lie on our bellies with our own rifles. Whoever the rider might be, he would be almost completely circled. The only escape route, to the rear, could be covered by our rifle fire.

Long minutes slid by while I felt that fierce sun burning the back of my neck. As I lay there, looking for a sign,

I felt like my eyeballs were starting to broil in my head. The silence was awesome, the only sound the occasional grinding of sand beneath one of our bodies as we changed position, seeking a more comfortable lie.

"Reckon he got smart an' circled 'round us?" Able Smith whispered, turning his head to glance at Slagle.

The sergeant only shook his head, continuing to squint against the sun's glare, facing into the reflection of the near white dunes.

Then that black form topped the ridge, bobbing up and down. As it grew larger, I could see the horse was being driven hard. Even at that distance, it was evident the animal was about done in, its sides white with sweat foam.

"He's most killed that horse," Slagle muttered. The sergeant snaked his rifle forward, forcing the Colt's butt against his shoulder to stare across the iron sights, tracking the rider.

"You gonna shoot without knowin' who it is?" I demanded to know. What Slagle seemed about to do didn't seem right. But the decision was taken out of his hands in that moment. The foundering horse started down the face of the dune, then buckled at the knees. The animal pitched forward on its twisted neck, rolling down the height of loose sand. The rider, struggling to get clear of the animal, seemed to land on his shoulders, rolling over and over until he stopped at the bottom of the sandy depression.

The horse lay still for a moment, then began struggling, threshing the sand, but it couldn't gain its feet. Finally, it gave up and flopped back on its side, suddenly still. Slagle's rifle roared in my ear and I saw the horse jerk once, then seem to relax. Overhead, the buzzards were gathering, starting to circle lower. They always knew.

"Horse was done for," Able Smith declared, expressing

approval. Slagle ignored the comment, as he used the butt of his rifle to help himself to his feet.

"Let's see who he is," he ordered sharply, starting down the angled face of the sand dune to the dead horse and the crumpled figure that lay near it. The other drovers had risen and started toward us, but Smith motioned to them.

"Hold your positions!" he shouted. One at a time, they dropped back to their bellies, leveling their rifles at the figure lying dead-like in the sand. I wondered for an instant if I shouldn't be giving those orders, but secretly, I was glad Able Smith was with us.

The three of us half slid down the dune, pushing ankle-deep rivulets of sand ahead of us, then we crossed the floor of the ravine, where the wind had blown away most of the covering to leave a hard-packed, sun-cracked surface.

Slagle held his Colt six-shot carbine ready at his hip, muzzle trained on the dark figure. As we drew near, I could see the downed rider wore faded denim pants that were too large and a thin canvas coat. An old felt hat was pulled down hard over the hair. The figure, facedown and frail looking, seemed harmless enough. Nonetheless, Slagle kept that carbine muzzle trained on the beatdown black hat.

"Turn 'im over," he ordered me. "Let's take a look."

Still clutching my own rifle, I knelt to grab a shoulder, flipping the loose weight. It was surprisingly light.

The sun burned down on the quiet, unconscious features. I'd seen the face only a dozen hours earlier in the light of a smoky lantern. Slagle's voice was half snarl, half strangled disbelief.

"Damned, stupid woman!"

Chapter Six

Thurlow squinted at the sun lancing through the branches of the stunted willow and judged the time to be approaching noon. Realization of the time that had passed brought a slow rising of relief somewhere inside that he did not understand at first.

Hunkered in the green shadows, the lieutenant inspected that sense of relief, learning that he had dreaded the expectation of another ambush. Memory of the deliberate bushwhacking of that sergeant and his men still caused the bile to burn in his throat. Now the fact that the expected camel caravan had not arrived left him with a curious sense of satisfaction that he found disturbing. His mission was to capture camels, true, but he didn't approve of the tactics and felt out of his depth, helpless to control Todd Dixon and his cutthroats.

"They shoulda been here long before now," Rinker muttered. With Dixon, he was hunkered behind a downed tree a few yards away. Thurlow could hear their voices over the buzzing of insects that infested the undergrowth flanking the river.

At first glance, it was an unlikely place for an ambush

and that was why it had been selected. The area in which the three of them had taken up their waiting posts was swampy, even muddy in spots, and gnats rose in clouds when disturbed. Other men were scattered through the trees, too, while more of the guerrilla force were on the other side of the trail, hidden in positions along the high embankment.

This was one of the few places where the trail left the high ground that overlooked the river bed. The terrain above was cut with numerous ravines, which would make for poor going without moving miles inland toward the mountains. The first explorers probably had angled downward here to take advantage of the easier, more level ground. Since then, countless hooves and wagon rims had cut the trail deeper, wider.

A military mind might suspect an ambush from the bluffs overlooking the river, Thurlow mused, but would be less likely to expect anyone to choose to suffer the heat and infestation of the wooded strip along the banks of the Colorado. Yet, the positions in which Dixon had placed his motley, ragtag band provided a perfect interlocking pattern of crossfire.

The band had been led to the spot by Rinker, who was familiar with the country. Before the war, Rinker had been a prospector, criss-crossing this desert in his search for riches.

One night, lolling beside a campfire, the officer had questioned the man about his past. Rinker had said he was from Georgia. When the war had begun, he had found he had to choose a side. Georgia was a Confederate state. At first, he had planned to return East to join the Army of the Confederacy, but he didn't have a proper stake. Then he had met Todd Dixon.

Thurlow, new to the desert country then, had found Rinker interesting. Dixon was the leader of this rabble and he tended to rule with a heavy hand spiced with vague promises of plunder. Rinker, at the other extreme, seemed dedicated to the Southern cause. Thurlow had considered his quiet aloofness to be born of the time he had spent alone in the desert.

One morning at dawn, he had found Rinker standing on a cliff, staring out over the desert to the west. The officer had walked up behind him, aware that Rinker knew he was there, but the other hadn't turned to acknowledge his presence.

"See something out there?" Thurlow had asked.

"I've been seein' it as long as I've been in this country," was the quiet reply. Puzzled, Thurlow looked out across the desert and its patterns of colors that changed, shifted with the growing light.

"Ghosts?"

Rinker paused, then nodded thoughtfully. "S'pose you could call it a ghost. It's the ship of pearls."

"Ship of pearls?"

Rinker had swung toward him then, grinning self-consciously. "Prob'ly jest another tale, but the ol' Injuns tell about how that desert out there forty, fifty miles was part of the Gulf of Baja California a long time back. They's s'posed to have been a Spanish ship loaded with pearls floatin' around out there. There come a big earthquake an' when it was over, the ship was trapped. Them Spaniards sailed round an' round, lookin' for a way out. Finally, they run the ship aground an' just took off 'cross the desert headed south, lookin' for their own people. Injuns say that ship's still out there, buried by sand dunes most times. But comes a storm, they say it gets uncovered for a while. Then the next storm covers it up again."

Rinker paused, shaking his head, looking back to the endless rippling sands. "It's been seen, they say, but it ain't never been by me." It was the most Thurlow had ever heard him say. Most of the time Rinker said little and answered in monosyllables.

"You've been seeking that ship ever since you came out here?"

"Not all the time. I found a bit of gold from time to time, but never enough to get rich. Found a lot more Injuns 'n' gold out there. Apaches. Yaquis. Yumas. They tend to put a crimp in gold-seekin'!" Rinker waved his hand at the subtle glow of the desert. "There's gold in most all the dry streambeds an' along the river, if a body wants to wash out three, four tons of sand just to see a speck of color in the bottom of his pan."

Dixon had approached soundlessly, to interrupt.

"Let's get movin'." His words had been more an order than a suggestion, and Russell Thurlow had recognized the fact that Dixon disliked the idea of his becoming too friendly with any of the renegades. But the young officer had felt for a few moments that he had been allowed to see into the soul of the grizzled prospector. He had thought fleetingly that he might have found an ally, until he had seen Rinker level his rifle and shoot the Yankee off the back of the lead camel in that first ambush. Too, it had been Rinker who had suggested scalping the Yankee soldiers and leaving them lie for the buzzards and the coyotes. Now, in spite of his revulsion, he realized Rinker knew Indians and he might better have taken the advice pushed at him by the prospector and Dixon instead of having the ambushed soldiers buried. Still, there were differences. Dixon seemed to revel in killing, feeding on the blood and excitement. Rinker approached it as a distasteful job that still required perfection in its performance.

"They coulda got a late start," Dixon said. "We'll give 'em a few more minutes."

"We should give it up for now," Thurlow declared. He kept his tone low, but summoned a hardness to his voice that he hoped served as command presence. "They'll likely be on guard against another ambush so soon. Especially if they didn't believe it was Indians." By casting doubt, he realized he was admitting he had been wrong about the burial.

Dixon's voice was chiding. "That ain't no way to think, Lootenant. You want camels, they got 'em."

"And they have gold, if your spy is correct." The young Confederate could not keep the accusation out of his tone. "But if there's enough to be worthwhile, how could they carry that much on a camel?"

"They got it hid somewhere in them supplies." There was an edge to Dixon's tone. He didn't like being questioned or doubted by one so young, even if he was an officer. The renegade also had recognized the accusation in his voice. During the ride to this ambush site, Thurlow had come to realize Todd Dixon was much more interested in gold than in fulfilling the mission of capturing camels for the Confederacy. Now the outlaw realized he was aware.

Hunkered in the shading underbrush, Russell Thurlow allowed his mind to wander, considering his own well being. He should attempt to get away from this band of cutthroats and, for a moment, he wondered whether he might be able to retreat southward through the brush, then cross the trail to the bluffs unseen. He might be able to circle around to the horses, surprise the guard and take one of the mounts. But as the thought formed, he knew he was thinking in terms of desertion and quickly cleansed the fantasy from his mind.

"Reckon they've outsmarted us, Todd." Rinker straightened from his position, moving his shoulders back and forth as though to relieve a cramp. He had been in a crouch with a rifle leveled across a branch, but now he set the long gun aside and holstered the revolver that had been ready near his hand. "Either they ain't comin' or they cut a new trail."

Dixon didn't like admitting defeat to an underling. Finally, though, he rose, holstering his big handgun, with a shake of his head.

"Maybe so." He glanced toward Thurlow's position and raised his voice a bit. "We'll get the horses, then see whether we can cut their trail. They'd hafta be on the California side." He jerked his head toward the bluffs and the brown mountains beyond. "That country's too rough for 'em to move with much speed an' they'd be even more suspicious of ambush in them canyons."

From where he stood in the willows, Thurlow saw Rinker give Dixon a long, hard look. Then the prospector shrugged and began edging out of the swamp, picking his way. The others fell in behind him, coming out of the trees one by one.

"The buzzards just think they've outsmarted me," Dixon growled, as the renegades gathered in the depression where the horses were hidden. He turned toward Rinker as though to issue an order, but the bearded prospector already was swinging into the saddle of his own buckskin mount. Without a word, rifle balanced across his saddle in front of him, he spurred his horse down the ravine toward the river.

"Have you considered that they may be traveling the other side of the river so they can draw us out into the open for a fight?" Thurlow had hunkered down beside Dixon in the shade of a manzanita. The guerrilla cast him a superior glance, waving a hand at his nearly two dozen men.

"What chance'd they have?" he demanded. "There was no more'n ten camels in that camp last night. Even if'n they all come downtrail, they'd be no match."

The guerrillas certainly had the Yankees outgunned,

but Thurlow was less than impressed with Dixon's ideas of tactics. He was the type who would bull into a fight and trust to win simply with more firepower. Thus far, though, he had been outthought and outmaneuvered.

Some of the band were checking their horses, while others clustered in the shade supplied by the ravine's overhang. One brought out a deck of greasy cards and a circle of poker players gathered about.

Aware that arguing with Todd Dixon would gain him only further contempt, Thurlow leaned back against the manzanita and pulled his sombrero low over his eyes, cutting out the sun. He watched a desert scorpion as it came forward to inspect his boot sole.

He hadn't meant to sleep and was surprised when a rough hand shook his shoulder. He shoved back his hat and glanced about, not knowing for an instant where he was. The shadows had grown longer in the canyon and the scorpion was gone.

"Rinker's comin' in," Dixon growled, rising. Thurlow struggled to his feet, stretching. His position in sleep had left him stiff in the shoulders.

The Georgian's horse was sweaty, flecked with foam, and was moving slowly. The rider came up the ravine and drew weary rein to slide from the saddle. The others had risen, too, the cards disappearing, but Rinker ignored them, as he unslung his canteen from his saddle horn, removed his battered hat and poured water into it. He stepped to his horse's head and thrust the hat in front of its nose. The spent animal drank noisily, then looked up at his owner as though asking for more. Rinker slapped the felt against his leg to remove the excess moisture, then settled the hat deliberately on his head.

Dixon, irritated at seemingly being deliberately ignored, stalked across the opening. "Did you find 'em?"

Rinker turned, surveying his leader with disinterested

eyes. Finally, as Dixon halted, legs spread before him, he nodded. "I found 'em. Someone else was followin' 'em an' they shot him."

"But who?" Thurlow wanted to know, puzzled. "Just one rider?"

Rinker nodded again, glancing at the lieutenant, at the same time making it obvious he was ignoring Dixon. "One rider," he affirmed. "They killed his horse an' him, too. I was on top of the ridge when they was all gathered around the corpse."

"We should've all gone," one of the riders protested. "That'd been the time to take 'em."

"Maybe so," Rinker agreed, "but we'd best hurry, if we're gonna get our chance."

"What's that mean?" Dixon demanded.

Rinker turned and pointed down the canyon. The wasteland across the river was not visible from their position and at first Thurlow thought they were only small clouds in the burning sky. But then he realized the ball-like puffs were rising rapidly in the still, hot air. Smoke!

"Apaches. They've seen them Yankees," the prospector said. "An' prob'ly us, too."

Chapter Seven

I poured water from my canteen over the girl's head and she began to move. Then, kneeling beside her, I pulled her up enough that I could pour a trickle down her throat. She gagged, then began to cough. I poured some more water over her bare head and she shook it off like a dog does after coming out of a pond. Her curls were gone, her hair plastered to her head. Still not fully conscious, she looked sort of small and forlorn.

But that didn't keep her from showing her anger. I was about to dowse her again, when she squinted up at me, eyes narrowed against the sun. "That's enough. Stop it."

I got up on my feet and stepped back to cap the canteen, while she groped in the sand until her hand found her battered hat. Her eyes were closed against the sun, I noted, or I'd maybe have thought she was blind. She pulled the beat-up old felt down over her wet head, then tried to get up. I made like to help her, but Slagle motioned me back. She was on her knees when she saw the dead animal splayed out at the bottom of the sand dune she'd tried to ride down.

"What'd you do to my horse?" It was near to a scream, showing the panic she must be feeling.

"I shot him!" Slagle told her. It came out sort of cynical-like, as though he was savoring a job well done. The girl looked up at him, eyes blazing in her pinched, white face.

"You shot him!" She repeated his words as though wanting him to say it again and she was leading him on. Slagle was quick to agree.

"I shot him." He returned her glare. "But you killed him. Run him to death."

The girl sort of sank back, sitting on her heels, staring at her dead mount, maybe realizing for the first time she was in the middle of a desert with no transport save her own feet.

"Lady, just who the hell are you?" Slagle demanded. I noted then that he was holding his Colt carbine so the muzzle was pointed at her breastbone. It wasn't like it was a deliberate aim, but it wasn't the sort of thing a sergeant who knew about firearms was likely to do without good reason.

"O'Roark. Elizabeth O'Roark." She still stared at the dead horse, as though trying to wish life back into the carcass.

"Why was you follerin' us?"

The girl look up at Slagle, seeming sort of surprised he'd ask such a question. "I told you I have to get to Yuma. I knew if I followed you, I'd get there."

Slagle shook his head. "Not without a horse, you won't."

"You're United States soldiers and I'm engaged to marry Sergeant Tuppy. Doesn't that mean anything?" There was accusation in the Irish lilt of her voice, as though to tell us we had just run out of gentlemen. But the panic I'd seen was in her eyes again, too.

"I suppose it has to mean something." Slagle's tone was grudging, but I noted that the muzzle of his carbine dropped to point at the sand. I was wondering whether he was going to tell her what had happened to Dan Tuppy, when he added, "But no lady's got any business out here in the desert on her own."

I'd always tend to think of a lady as someone that's high-born, knows how to carry on small talk, and wears fancy dresses. I was thinking then that, if those things were really what it took to quality for ladyhood, Elizabeth O'Roark was being misidentified by the sergeant. Kneeling there in her rough clothes, her beat-up hat and her water-soaked hair, she looked like a twelve-year-old orphan that'd been dragged out of the creek after trying to do away with herself. I couldn't help but feel sorry for her.

"She ain't on her own," I muttered. "We're here." That got me nothing better than a dirty look from Sergeant Slagle.

"What's to make us think you ain't a spy for the Johnny Rebs?" Slagle demanded, tone hard again.

"Do I look like a spy, Sergeant?" Her tone threw off a lot more chill than one could expect in the desert heat. She held a hand out to me. "Help me up, please."

I glanced at Sergeant Slagle and he sort of dipped his chin, just enough to let me know I wasn't likely to get court-martialed right away for consorting with the enemy. When I took the girl's hand, her fingers felt soft and cool to my touch in spite of the temperature and the ordeal she'd just been through.

"Where're you from, Miss O'Roark?" I asked, as she took off her hat and began to comb her fingers through her hair. It was sort of red in color, about the same shade as a sorrel horse. Then she began to brush the sand off her clothes.

"Boston. At least, that's where I worked these past three years."

"Where'd you live in the Old Country?" Slagle wanted to know. He, too, had recognized the Irish lilt in her tone.

"County Cork. That was where Dan Tuppy was from, too."

I noted that Slagle stiffened a trifle and knew he had caught her reference to the past. Did she know Tuppy was dead or was she simply saying he had come from Ireland before he had come to this country to join up with the cavalry? If she realized she had made any sort of slip, it didn't show in her face. She nodded her thanks to me, then turned back to Slagle.

"What are you going to do with me?" she wanted to know, suddenly showing the sort of self-assurance that had been evident the night before when she had come to the camel camp.

Slagle was eyeing her over with a sort of speculation. When she was standing, it was obvious she was a woman, not a girl. The rough shirt she wore was pushed out by her breasts and she'd had to pull the belt up tight to keep the too-big pants from falling off. Even in that outfit, she was shapely enough to keep me looking. Slagle, too.

"If I was even half smart, I'd leave you here, but I don't reckon that'd be thought gentlemanly back in County Cork. You ever ride a camel?" She started to answer, but he cut her off. "You ever been bad seasick?"

The girl acted sort of indignant, as though it was a fool question. "Sergeant, I sailed from Ireland to Boston through a big storm. Then I came clear around the Horn to San Francisco. I don't get seasick!"

"Interestin' to hear." Slagle sounded downright mild

and I could see he was trying not to grin. "All your sea-goin' experience should prove a real benefit."

"Sam, we'd best quit all this palaver and get down the trail," Able Smith put in suddenly. "We're likely to be meetin' up with some bad company."

The grizzled corporal was staring off over the top of one of the sand dunes that rose above us. The other troopers up on the crest were standing, too, clutching the lead ropes on their camels. They were looking in the same direction, moving nervously.

"Apache war smoke," Smith decreed, watching the white plume that rose into the silent, burning sky. "An' you kin bet they know where we are!"

Chapter Eight

"I'll bet another ten on my aces."

"I'm out. Too steep for me," one of the renegades growled, and threw in his cards. Four of them were in the game, one dealing from the greasy deck, while Thurlow watched with growing anger. They seemed far more interested in their game than the mission.

But Russell Thurlow knew, too, that it would do no good to say anything to them. They followed Dixon and they did what he told them to do. The officer realized that some of the renegades—and he had reached the conclusion they were exactly that—resented him. He had seen it in their expressions. Others tended to view him with silent, covert amusement, aware that he was out of his depth. The desert killing grounds were no place for a fancy-pants young lieutenant not long off a Southern plantation. Thurlow had seen that feeling in their eyes.

Resolutely, the young officer whirled and stalked through the protective ring of boulders to where Dixon lay, hat pulled down over his face. In spite of the gang leader's prone position, his right hand rested on the butt of the odd-looking LeMatt pistol. Thurlow noted that

Dixon's finger was extended through the trigger guard, resting lightly upon the trigger.

"Dixon!" He felt the urge to toe the man in the ribs with his boot, but decided against it. No telling what the other's reaction might be to being rudely awakened.

"What'cha after, soldier boy?" Dixon had been awake all along, Thurlow realized, and no doubt had been fully aware of his approach. The renegade reached up with his free hand to slide the hat off his face, the right hand never leaving the gun butt. The slighting reference to his status did not go unnoted by Lieutenant Thurlow, but he squatted beside the other, seeking the shade.

"Why aren't we doing something instead of just staying holed up here in the heat and rocks?" Thurlow tried to make his expression stern.

Dixon offered a sigh and sat up slowly, staring into Thurlow's eyes. The officer saw the same contempt that he had noted among the others. Until now, Dixon had kept it under control, but suddenly there seemed to be no reason for further deception.

"The big trouble with all you Southern gentlemen is you don't know how to wait. You gotta rush out there an' cross swords to prove what big heroes you—"

"Mister Dixon, I don't need nor appreciate your opinions of the South and Southerners." Thurlow was smarting beneath the insult and realized he was allowing his anger to get in the way of common sense. "I want to know about your plan of action. What are we going to do to capture those camels?"

Dixon lowered his head to spit into the dust. The ball of tobacco-stained moisture landed between Thurlow's knees.

"Considerin' that you're only payin' five hundred dollars apiece for them animals, you're askin' for an awful lotta service, mister."

"That's why I was sent here," Thurlow declared stubbornly. "And when I hired you, it was agreed that you and your men would do what had to be done."

Dixon heaved another exaggerated sigh as though he found it a burden to cope with one so young and inexperienced.

"We got two problems, Lootenant. First off, you seen that Apache war smoke. If they ain't seen us, then that means they're prob'ly after them blue bellies an' their camels the same as us.

"Right now, I got two men out scoutin'. Their first interest is to locate them Injuns an' see what they're up to. An' they're also to find them camels. They could be anywhere in this desert. Meantime, we ain't too bad off here an' we're savin' water an' our horses."

When it had been discovered that the camel train was not on the Arizona side of the Colorado and was not following the well-used trail Tuppy and his band had taken, Dixon had ordered a long, hard march to the south. His reasoning had been that the horses could move faster than the camels and, by pushing hard, they could get ahead of the slow-moving treasure train. In Russell Thurlow's mind, a treasure train was exactly what the caravan had become in the thoughts of the others. If gold really was being carried by the desert beasts, Dixon and his men would be much more interested in such a cache than in the few hundred dollars they could collect for capturing Yankee camels.

"You're sure we're ahead of the Yankees?" the officer asked, hoping his eyes did not betray his understanding of what was taking place. A show of ignorance seemed the safest policy.

Dixon nodded and spit more tobacco juice. "I'd bet on it. In fact, if them blue bellies seen them smoke signals, they may be forted up somewhere, waiting to see what th' Apaches plan to do. That's what I'd do, if I was in their boots."

"It may be days before they reach us then." Thurlow was not fully satisfied with the explanation, although he understood the logic.

"Injuns don't like to attack at night," Dixon said, "but we ain't got no such compunctions. We'll find where they're camped. Then, if things go right, we can jump 'em in the dark. That'll maybe save some of my people from gettin' hurt. An' we can clear out before the Apaches get into the fracas."

"That's all I wanted. A reason for all this." Thurlow realized his acceptance had sounded lame, as he moved across the sandy clearing to where his horse was picketed.

"Don't mention it, sir," Dixon called after him. The exaggerated word of respect held the same note of contempt that had been evident throughout the conversation. Thurlow was pondering what Dixon had told him. He also had noted the mention of a fast escape ahead of the Apaches. That, he realized, meant Todd Dixon was considering only the gold, if there really was any. They would not be able to move rapidly, if they attempted to take the camels with them. The beasts could move fast enough, but in a running fight, they would surely prove a hindrance.

Russell Thurlow had realized that his chances of survival had been reduced as soon as Todd Dixon learned about the gold. As long as they had been after nothing but camels, he reasoned, the gang had to keep him alive so proper payment would be authorized. But if the Yankee caravan really was carrying gold and that was now Dixon's primary aim, Thurlow knew he would die. If they captured the gold, there no longer would be any need to keep him alive. And if they wanted to continue to milk the Confederacy with future projects, playing the role of a guerrilla force, they could not allow him to live to report what had happened.

Grimly considering his future, or lack of it, Russell Thurlow stretched out in the shade provided by the rocks and his horse, observing the others, wondering what thoughts might be going through each man's mind. Watching from beneath the brim of his sombrero, he saw Rinker leave the card game and join Dixon to hunker on his heels beside the gang leader. He was certain he was the subject of their conversation. Although he resented having to admit it even to himself, the vague grip of fear was clutching at his heart.

"General Lee givin' you some trouble?" Rinker asked quietly, removing his hat and running around the inner band to remove sweat.

Dixon offered a bleak smile. "Nothin' serious. He'll be gettin' hisself killed before he gets t'be too much of a nuisance."

Rinker shook his head, frowning. "I don't know 'bout him, Todd. He may look to be a dandy, but I've talked with him some. There's some steel in his spine that sorta gets hid by all them fancy words an' manners."

"He ain't got the guts. Trouble is he's too wrapped up in tryin' to be a hero to be any real problem. Besides, he knows what a hard bunch makes up Quantrill's outfit. He's walkin' careful with that in mind."

"Wonder what he'd think if he knew even Bill Quantrill couldn't abide havin' you around?" Rinker smiled thoughtfully and Dixon didn't like it.

"You ain't fixin' to tell him, are you? He'll know the truth before he dies." Todd Dixon was struck by a new thought. "Wonder what them Yankees pay for a spy if you deliver 'em one dead across his saddle?"

"Todd!"

The cry disrupted whatever Rinker might have said in

reply. The call was from the lone sentry posted atop one of the rocks.

"Scouts comin' in!" the sentry called, indicating the desert beyond by extending his arm, rifle in hand.

The scouts that Thurlow knew only as Finn and Hopkins rode in through the rocks, climbing wearily from their saddles. Their horses were wet with sweat and hollow-eyed with weariness, evidence that they had been ridden hard under the desert sun. The two riders were in little better shape.

Dixon spoke to Finn, but the big man shook his head impatiently and looked around until he found a canteen. He uncapped the container and removed his hat, pouring water into it. Then he held the headgear beneath his horse's nose until the animal plunged its mouth into the crown and began to drink. From where he sat, Thurlow watched, judging by Finn's treatment of his horse that the renegade had served as a horse soldier sometime in his life.

The other rider showed no interest in caring for his mount. He simply dropped the reins in a ground tie and unslung the canteen from his saddle to take a long draught, rinse it around in his mouth, then spit it into the sand before taking another drink.

Thurlow rose and strode across the clearing, as Finn, still holding the hat beneath his horse's nose, turned to look at Todd Dixon through swollen, red-rimmed eyes.

"What'd you find out there?" Dixon demanded, scowling.

"No Injuns. I reckon they're out there, but they ain't ready for us to see 'em yet," the renegade offered. "Nothin' but that smoke signal an' it didn't last long."

"The blue bellies? What about them?"

"They're comin' along about ten miles back. At the rate

they're movin', this is prob'ly where they intend to camp."

Dixon offered a tight nod. "They've camped here in the past." He glanced at Hopper disapprovingly. "Get that horse cooled out an' watered."

"If you're sure they plan to stop here, this would be the ideal place for an ambush," Thurlow suggested. Dixon ignored him, again centered his attention to Rinker.

"Jim, get the horses outta here, then have a coupla men get rid of our sign." He indicated a growth of desert bush half hidden in his rocks. "They can use that stuff to brush out the tracks. When that's done, get everyone set high up in the rocks. We'll have a little welcome for them blue bellies when they get here."

Rinker nodded and turned to the others who lolled about the area.

"A' wright! On your feet! Get them horses hid back outta sight an' pick up your gear." He motioned to two of the men. "You two. Do a sweep down an' get rid of all sign!" Rinker glanced at Thurlow almost apologetically. "You too, Lieutenant. Best get your horse hid out, then find yourself a good firin' position."

Russell Thurlow hesitated, casting a glance at Dixon. He resented being treated as an underling. But he nodded and moved off, Dixon staring after him. When the renegade spoke, his voice was low, meant only for Rinker.

"Keep an eye on that wet-ear, Jim. He don't cotton much to slaughter." He hesitated. "An' if he should get hisself shot, no one here's gonna grieve much."

Chapter Nine

"They call these monsters the ships of the desert." Sergeant Slagle kept his tone conversational sounding, but he glanced at the girl, trying to hide a grin. "Of course, all this here up an' down motion shouldn't bother an ol' salt that's sailed clear aroun' the Horn."

"If I wasn't so ill, I could find it easy to hate you, Sergeant." Beth O'Roark's words may have been menacing, but her voice was not. It was weak and miserable, sounding about the way she looked. She was perched behind Slagle on Big Red, and we'd traveled less than a mile, when she vomited the first time. There had been three more bouts of sickness, till she was retching with nothing but dry heaves. Her face was white as a wagon cover and she appeared to be having a good bit of trouble just hanging on, as the camel bounced along in its rippling stride. Through all this, Slagle'd been patently cheerful, pretending not to notice even when she just barely missed throwing up all over the leg of his uniform pants.

"Maybe it's a good thing you're sick then, miss". Slagle's tone was still bland, but I suspected he was enjoying his subtle tortures. "It's prob'ly savin' a beautiful friendship!"

"Oh shut up!" the girl snapped at him. She tried to straighten, but was still forced to clutch his pistol belt in order to maintain her balance on the back of the camel. "How much farther must we go?"

"To Yuma? It's a long piece yet. But jest for today, it ain't far. A few more miles an' we'll pitch camp in a spot I know."

A hundred yards or so up ahead, Able Smith pulled up his camel quick-like and raised his hand in signal for a halt. As I drew in my beast, I could see that the corporal was staring down at something in the sand.

Slagle growled at Big Red and the animal shuffled forward to be brought to a halt beside Able Smith, who already had signaled his mount to kneel and was hunkered over something he'd found in the sand.

I'd been told I was second in command and was curious. I edged my own camel out of the column and urged it up close enough to where I could see what it was that had attracted Able Smith's interest.

They were tracks. At least, that's what I took them to be. Actually, they were just impressions in the loose sand and already they had started to blow full, losing their shape. If they wasn't shadowed by the lowering sun, maybe Smith wouldn't have seen them at all.

"Looks like there was two of 'em," Able ventured. He dropped to one knee and picked up a handful of the loose sand from one of the imprints, letting it flow between his fingers. Slagle didn't bother to put his mount on its knees. He just swung a leg over the animal's neck and slid down its side to land on the ground beside Smith. He stared down at the tracks, then followed the fading trail with his eyes, scowling.

"Looks like they sat their horses here for a time and

watched us." He glanced about. The wind was picking up the way it does some evenings in the Mojave. "They wasn't here too long back or the wind woulda covered the tracks before now."

"If it's Apaches, we're in for a whole batch of trouble," Able Smith declared. His eyes were searching the skyline for any sign of movement. I looked, too, but there was nothing out there but the setting sun. Still, we'd all heard that old saying that, when you can't see an Apache, you'd best figure he's out there, figgering a way to make you die.

Slagle shook his head, the scowl still creasing his features. "If it's who I think it is, we're in for even bigger trouble." He shook his head again, as though trying to dispel his own concern. "That other caravan was ambushed and killed off just 'cause they wanted camels. We have ten camels here and we're also packin' ten thousand in gold!"

"Ten thousand?" Able Smith was awed by that big a figure and couldn't hide the fact. That was more than most men saw in a lifetime, especially if one was a soldier. "Where?"

"That keg of nails we had trouble strappin' down? It's fulla gold for the Yuma paymaster."

I was surprised that Slagle would lay it out in the open for everyone to hear. And I was just as surprised when he looked up at Beth O'Roark, still clinging to Big Red's skinny back.

"Sure wish I knew your part in alla this," he growled, accusation in his tone. Beth O'Roark just sat there, returning his stare as though not knowing what he meant or, at least, pretending. I noted, too, that Slagle had been mighty careful not to name Dan Tuppy when he'd talked about the slaughter of the other caravan. Sooner or later, somebody was going to have to tell Beth the true facts, if she didn't know already.

"No matter whether it's Apaches or Rebel raiders, we got troubles." Sam Slagle was staring ahead, eyeing the fast-dispappearing tracks. "If you was gonna spring an ambush on an outfit like this, where'd be the best spot to do it?"

Able Smith pondered for a moment, but I already knew the answer. I'd been this way before.

"The big rocks, I reckon." Nobody'd asked me, but I figured it was time I stuck my oar in. That was where Sam'd planned to night camp. "Be plumb easy to jump us there."

Slagle nodded thoughtfully, giving me a glance that was about as close as he was ever likely to show in the way of approval.

"Right. So we're gonna swing east to the mountains, then cut back towards the fort."

"But we don't have enough water for that!" Smith protested.

"We gotta cross back over the river," Slagle declared. "We'll fill up then."

I lost track of time. Had there been a moon, I'd have had some idea of the hours that passed, but there was only the lonesome brightness of the stars. They cast off just enough light to make every bush look like an Indian, every rill in the sand a likely place for a renegade to be hiding. I don't like to admit I was scared, but I must have been. I was plumb worn out from the strain by the time Sam Slagle found a likely place to camp. It was up the mouth of a narrow arroyo where we'd be protected from the wind and blowing sand. We had filled our canteens and let the camels drink before we had crossed the Rio Colorado to end up on the Arizona side. But instead of simply wading our animals across and picking up the familiar trail, Slagle had led us up the streambed a good three miles, keeping the camels knee deep in the scummy, odorous water to hide their tracks. It wasn't a new trick by any means, but it might serve to confuse whoever was after us for a time.

Since the sand back there in the desert had been too loose and windblown to hold a print, we still didn't know whether the horses of the two who'd been spying on us were shod. Had we been able to tell, we'd have had a better idea whether it was Apaches or raiders. Indians might ride a horse wearing iron, if he's just stolen it, but when the shoes wear out, they ride barefoot from then on. Their own ponies are never shod, of course.

There in the arroyo, we staked out the camels where they could feed on some of the sparse vegetation. Normally, we would have offloaded the supplies and saddles, but this time, Slagle decided against it. There was no telling when we might have to make a run for it and he wanted to be ready.

We built no fire and, as we searched out areas to tie the beasts where they wouldn't get tangled up in each others picket ropes, Able Smith kept glancing toward the girl. She'd found a flat bed of sand without any brush and was trying to make a comfortable bed, spreading the blanket I'd given her.

"You figger her showin' up to marry Dan Tuppy the day after he got killed isn't coincidence?" Able asked Slagle, keeping his voice low so the girl and the others couldn't hear. Slagle offered a shake of his head, showing a grimace that I'd best describe as frustration.

"Hell, I don't know what to think. For certain, I don't trust her, but I ain't got time to worry over it now." He cast me a sidelong glance that I didn't like. I'd seen that look before, mostly in saloons just before Slagle went into the wrecking business. "Wagner, she seems to fancy your manners. Why don't you just wander over there to be certain she's gonna be comfortable for the night. You might get her to talking."

I didn't like the idea of playing spy on a woman, but I couldn't come up with any other acceptable reason against what amounted to a direct order. Still, I put as much disrespect as I dared in my acknowledgement. "Whatever the sergeant wants."

"You'll go far in this man's army with a positive attitude like that, Corporal." Slagle made this announcement with a pretended heartiness. He'd recognized I was being deliberately disrespectful and turned it back on me. I pondered later about how he'd managed to make me feel mean and small right then, but he'd had a whole batch of practice at it over his years.

Beth O'Roark was hunkered on her blanket, knees drawn up so she could rest her chin on them, while she listened to the grumbling going on among the troopers a few yards away. If she found it amusing, it didn't show on what I could see of her face there in the growing night.

Sid Jordan already was wrapped up in his blankets and was using a camel saddle for a pillow, his hat wadded as a cushion against the leather-covered hardwood frame.

"I'll never be able to brag to my grandchildren," he muttered to no one in particular, as he burrowed against the blanket's rough wool, trying to form a hole in the sand beneath that his long, angular figure would fit. "When they ask what I did in this here war, there ain't no way I can admit I was nursemaid to a camel."

I paused beside him, not wanting to make so direct an approach to the girl. If I was supposed to find out things from her, there was no reason to make her suspicious as a start.

"The camels're here for a purpose, Sid, just like you

an' me," I told him, loud enough for the girl to hear. "Just 'cause maybe President Lincoln ain't sent us his personal word of explanation don't mean we ain't doin' some good for the Union."

Jordan rolled over part way to look up at me with a baleful stare. "I declare, kid, I think you actually like these mange-infested beasts. You've been stayin' too close to Sergeant Slagle. He thinks the sun rises an' sets on that red creature. Me, I don't trust none of 'em enough to ever turn my back on 'em. I joined the cavalry 'cause they got horses. If I was s'posed to be a camel jockey, I'd of been born an Arab!"

"Go to sleep, Sid. It'll all look better in the mornin'," one of the other troopers growled. Jordan was interfering with his own thoughts or perhaps his sleep.

I moved over to where the girl still sat, arms clasped around her knees. "Want some help gettin' your boots off, miss?"

She looked up seeming surprised at my offer, then gave me the edge of a smile. "That's kind of you, Corporal. I was considering sleeping in them."

"No, ma'am," I protested. "No one sleeps well if their feet're all pinched up. It's sort of like pinchin' your soul an' you'll never sleep."

That brought a little laugh from her and she unfolded her arms, extending one leg so I could grab the boot by the toe and the heel to work it off. The heavy leather finally came free with a sort of sucking sound. At least, I thought, her boots fit proper, which was more than could be said for the rest of her clothes. Someone told me once that you know a boot fits right when you're able to get it off just before you go full unconscious from the effort.

I took the other boot off the same way and carefully lined them up in the sand at the bottom of her blanket.

"There. You'll be able to find 'em even in the dark, if you hafta," I told her.

"You might sit down and keep me company for a while, unless you're tired," she suggested in that prim Irish tone. "Nobody else has much to say to me. They think I'm a spy." I was sort of embarrassed by the invite, and I could see she knew it and was trying not to laugh at me.

"I thought, bein' sick like you was, you'd want to sleep."

She shook her head, smiling full this time. "Not yet." She patted the blanket beside her hip. "Sit down. We really haven't had much chance to talk."

She was right about that. I'd been riding abreast of her and Slagle for a time. She'd tried to be conversational and had explained to us both that her name was Elizabeth, but nearly everyone called her Beth. She'd been cheerful enough, it seemed, at being rescued and joining up with us.

But it was only minutes after that when her stomach started to pitch against the rhythm of Big Red's rolling stride and sickness got her. I'd found myself being embarrassed over her efforts to seem strong, gagging behind Sam Slagle's back, till finally she couldn't keep it down anymore. I'd drawn back and pulled my camel into line behind Sid Jordan's.

"You're name's Wagner. I know that much," she said, as I settled on the edge of the blanket, one buttock in the sand, taking care not to get close to her. "What's your first name?"

"Jeff. Jeffery, ma'am."

There was a hint of a chuckle. "Don't you think we should dispense with the ma'am, Jeff? After all, we'll be spending a lot of time together, out here under the same stars."

I gulped, wondering just what she was trying to say. I'd not had all that much to do with girls and back home, with my own sisters, I'd never been full sure what they meant, when they just appeared foolish in their prattle.

"Why are we going back?" she wanted to know suddenly, lowering her voice. "Are we being followed?"

I didn't know how much I should tell her. "There's Apaches on the prowl an' we saw them tracks. Sergeant Slagle figgers they might be white renegades, maybe even Rebel guerrillas, if they ain't Injuns."

"Or it could be a patrol from Fort Yuma coming to escort you in," she suggested. "Isn't that possible?"

I shook my head. "Not likely. They wouldn't come this far north."

"And it couldn't be Dan Tuppy and his caravan headed for Fort Mojave, could it?" Her tone was innocent enough, but I felt she was hemming me in.

"Don't reckon."

"You all seem to know Dan, but nobody wants to talk about him," She was pushing now, her voice low but hard. "What's happened to him, Jeff?"

I didn't say anything for a moment. "Maybe you'd best talk to the sergeant 'bout this sort of thing," I said finally.

"He's dead, isn't he, Jeff?" Her voice was toneless with pain, maybe I expected to hear anger and outrage. There was none. "He's been dead all along and no one would tell me!"

Chapter Ten

I'd not been around a lot of young women in my life, so I didn't really know what I expected of Beth O'Roark. I thought maybe she'd cry or throw some sort of tantrum, but she didn't do neither. She just dropped her head and seemed to stare at the hands that she suddenly folded in her lap. It was almost like she was in a daze. Or maybe saying a silent prayer.

"How did it happen, Jeff?" Her voice was quiet but demanding, her eyes on her hands.

"You'd best talk to Sergeant Slagle 'bout that, ma'am."

"I don't want to talk to Slagle. I'm talking to you!" There was anger in her, too, but I figured that for a product of grief. I'd seen that sort of reaction a number of times, when I was coming West.

I'd been somewhere around the age of fifteen near as I've ever been able to reckon, when I ran away and joined up with a wagon train that was headed for California. I figured anything and any place had to be better than where I was.

My childhood was sort of a muddle. I had only a vague recollection of my early years, most of it in an orphanage, where there sometimes wasn't enough to eat and where two or three of us slept in the same bed on winter nights just to keep warm. The dormitory, as they called it, was a big bare room heated by a single coal stove. The fire always was allowed to go out right after the evening meal so as to save money, the thirty of us crowded together to share our misery.

The blankets wasn't all that thick neither, so we huddled together beneath them at night, sharing our body warmth, hoping morning would come soon. It might not be much warmer even then, but we'd each of us know we'd made it through another night. Some of the kids didn't even manage that. Sometimes, one would catch pneumonia or some other disease and die in the darkness, surrounded but still alone.

We got some schooling at the orphanage, but I never did learn to read or write much and ciphering was an art I never did get the proper hang of. The minute any kind of arithmetic class started, I figured I already was at least two weeks behind everyone else.

The summers took care of the cold right enough, but they were a real burden for us kids. The orphanage didn't get a lot of county money and it was up to us to raise enough to feed ourselves and hope to store up enough extra to see us through the winter months. The orphanage people would hire one of the nearby farmers every spring to plow the ground nearby. That's all he'd do. Then all of us, boys and girls alike, would be out there, using steel-toothed rakes to knock down the clods and smooth out the dirt for planting. The ground was mostly sand and didn't grow anything well. We did have a few cows and some chickens, though, and we'd clean out the barn and henhouses before the plow went into the ground, scattering the manure around the plots by hand, flinging it from buckets, but even that didn't seem to help much. The stuff we planted seemed to take more out of the soil than we was ever able to put back into it. Each year, the crop was a little skimpier and there was less to keep us through the winter.

Most kids would've thought themselves lucky to have someone to adopt them and, when Mrs. Wagner came to collect me, I maybe felt that way. I don't rightly recall, though I must've been about twelve or so at the time. What I did learn right soon was that you didn't have to be black to be treated as a slave.

The woman ran a restaurant in town and she needed a lackey she didn't have to pay to do the dishwashing, swab out the place, carry wood and coal, and shovel snow. I'd expected I'd maybe be treated as one of the family, taking my place with her two daughters, in the scheme of things, but that dream got disrupted right off.

When there was company or we was in church, Mrs. Wagner acted as though she really thought well of me and insisted I act as though I felt her daughters were my sisters. That, I figured, was to impress the preacher and her eating-house customers.

When no one was around, I was made to sleep in the basement beneath the restaurant and I had to be up before daylight each day to set the cooking fires, see that the water was bucketed in from the pump, and that all of the tables was set proper.

That basement was damp and cold in the winter, frost sticking to the brick walls, and several times I came down with bad colds. Being sick didn't cut no ice with the Wagner woman, though, and she wasn't above saying she'd ship me back to the orphanage, if I didn't do exactly as she said and do it right quick.

That went on for near onto three years, while I got my growth at about the same rate I developed a hate for her and her prissy daughters. Finally, when I'd had enough,

I cleaned out her cash box one night and ran off, making my way out of Southern Illinois, across the Mississippi River and up to St. Joe, where I knew the wagon trains made up to head west.

I tried to sign on with several wagon trains that I saw making up there, but no one took me serious, telling me flat out that I was too young to be of much account. Finally, though, an old wagonmaster named Teech put me on to help herd the livestock. A place to sleep beneath a wagon at night and enough to eat was what he considered fair pay and I wasn't in much position to argue with him.

It took us near to eight months to cross the nation and I eventually skinned off in the California mountains and made for San Francisco, where I thought they'd been finding all the gold. I had ideas of being a miner, but I soon found there was no gold on the Barbary Coast and I near starved to death before someone told me they was enlisting soldiers at Fort Alcatraz. I was able to take a boat out there to the island and signed my name to an enlistment.

There were others no older than myself who'd enlisted, too, but I was a couple up on most of them. I'd grown some and seasoned out during that trip with the wagon train. I'd also been in a couple of battles with Plains Indians and I'd learned to fire a rifle under heavy pressure, since the redskins was shooting back.

I learned all the soldiering basics like drilling and polishing gear to a high shine, and took part in the hit-and-miss training. Then, when they figured I knew enough, they shipped me off to Fort Defiance in Arizona, where our main duty was supposed to be to control the Navajos in the area.

I got assigned to the First Dragoons, a horse outfit, and did a lot of riding and mighty little fighting. The Navajos had been a warlike tribe in their time, I reckon, but after a final big battle with the Apaches, they had settled into farming the area around the fort, where there was good land and sufficient water.

It was boring and short on excitement, but maybe for the first time in my life, I felt like I had a home and took to cavalry life like a duck to water. In fact, I began to take a sort of proprietary pride in the fort, till the word came down that it was to be abandoned. Most of the garrison was shipped off to Fort Fauntleroy in New Mexico, which would put them a bit closer to the War Between the States that seemed to be burning up the East.

But my own orders was different. I was assigned to Fort Yuma, which I always thought of as another cavalry post. Instead, it turned out to be a quartermaster depot, where supplies was stocked after being brought up the Colorado River from the Gulf of Lower California. It was also where I'd been signed up with the camel outfit and first met Sergeant Slagle and some of the others.

At first, I tried to talk my way out of the assignment. I told anyone that'd listen that I didn't even like camels, but that didn't mean much. It turned out no one else liked them either.

I didn't think much about it then or maybe I didn't even know it, but in looking back, I guess I tended to be something of a loner. Most of the troopers I'd known along the way seemed content just to live from payday to payday, celebrating the end of every month with a bad-whiskey hangover, then they'd start all over again to build up another head of buried frustration till they got paid and could do it all over again.

I tended to stick to myself a lot and learned some reading, when I could find or borrow books. A lot of the troopers thought I was sort of sissified, since I wasn't out throwing my money away in saloons and cat houses. Truth is, I liked being around the barracks and the stables, when I wasn't on the trail. A cavalry post was as close as I'd ever been to having a home and there was a warmth and a sense of security inside the compound that made me feel good, maybe even protected. Whatever the reasons, I tended to mind my own business, do as I was told, and work to stay out of the guard house. Maybe that's why I got my corporal's stripes a long time before some oldtimers figured I really was ready for them.

And maybe all of this was why I was the one Beth O'Roark wanted to have tell her what had happened to Dan Tuppy. She might not have been a loner as such, but she surely was alone out there in the sun and sand. She may have sensed that we had something in common; some sort of bond that the others wouldn't understand. The thought occurred to me at the time that she was talking to me because I was the youngest and wouldn't have the facility to side-step her questions.

"I want you to tell me what happened to Dan Tuppy," she insisted. Her voice was low and rough-sounding, like she was fighting to keep back the tears. Her eyes still was focused on the hands folded in her lap and I could see no evidence of tears. In fact, there was a brittleness about her now that I found bothersome.

I was certain Slagle and the others were watching and I kept my voice low, not wanting to be overheard. There was no real reason, except that I felt I was in the middle of a situation, where I couldn't win and I didn't need no critics at that moment.

I told Beth O'Roark about how Tuppy and his caravan had been ambushed and killed, then the camels driven off.

"But weren't the bodies brought back to the fort?" she demanded, looking up at me, frowning through what appeared to be cold anger. "Where they could be given decent burial?"

"No, ma'am." I shook my head. "They was buried out there where they was found. That's the way things happen in the desert. Bodies tend to putrefy in an almighty hurry. It's best for all concerned to commit 'em to the ground fast."

Her anger turned to a sort of horror or maybe it was simply revulsion at the words I'd chosen to explain the situation. Thinking back, I reckon I must have sounded pretty heartless, though I didn't mean to seem so.

"Dan Tuppy was a Catholic," she said. "He needs to be buried in a cemetery, in hallowed ground, if his soul is to be saved."

"We ain't got many priests out here, ma'am, but what I know of the frontier, if a man's buried where he dies, that's considered hallowed ground enough by your church. The priests must figger even God has to make some allowances for circumstance."

That was when the tears came. There was no sound, just the streams of dampness coursing down her cheeks. She made no attempt to wipe them away. For a moment, I was tempted to use my scarf to dry her face, but I realized Slagle and the others would be watching. I'd hear about it later, I knew.

Also, I didn't know a blessed thing about her priests and how the Roman Catholic Church felt about people being buried in the desert. What I'd told her just seemed to be born of common sense. At least, it made sense to me.

It was full dark by then and I didn't figure Slagle and the others would be able to see. I reached out to take one of the girl's hands, wrapping my fingers around it. In spite of the heat that still came at us from the sand and the rocks, her skin was cold, sort of clammy to my touch. I don't know how long we sat there before I realized a pair of boots was planted right in front of me.

"Miss O'Roark, you'd best try to get some sleep," Sam Slagle suggested. There was a gruffness in his tone that suggested he hadn't changed his thoughts much. He still figured maybe she was a spy. Without thinking, I drew my hand away, looking up at him.

"Let her be, Sergeant." There was an anger in my tone that I found surprising. But maybe I recognized her fear and her loneliness. I'd experienced enough of my own over the years. I'd reckoned, too, that we were about the same age and that there maybe was something that sort of drew us together.

"You've got the first watch, Corporal. Better get posted," Sam Slagle growled and turned to walk away. I hesitated, looking at the girl again, but if she was still crying in that silent way of hers, I couldn't tell. Her face was just sort of a blur in the darkness.

"Be careful, Jeffery." Her tone was soft, almost pleading that I take extra precautions.

"I will," I promised as I heaved to my feet. "Moon'll be up soon. Ain't nobody gonna slip up on us in the dark." I looked down at her. "Do like Sergeant Slagle said. Get some sleep. Tomorrow's likely to be a hard day."

"Worse than this one?" There was a strange irony in her voice.

Chapter Eleven

I sat hunkered down in the rocks with a mesquite bush to my back so as to break up the outline of my body, while I was staring out into the night. I was on guard at the entrance to the little arroyo, where we'd settled in for the night. A thinning moon had come up and by its light, I could see out across the desert sand for what seemed miles. In the distance, I could see the darkness of mountains that flanked the desert to the west. The moon was down to the last quarter, but the light it shed seemed to bounce off the sand and offer up a strange, ghost-like brilliance.

There was an odd sort of beauty to the soft brightness and it had a lulling effect that might tend to hypnotize a man, if he wasn't aware of the danger and guarded against it. Over the years, I'd stood a lot of such watches and had learned how to keep awake. In spite of that, I caught myself nodding off once and jerked my head up quick enough. I stuck my tongue between my teeth and bit down on it deliberate like, feeling the pain, tasting it, until it brought me full awake. That would last a time, then I'd have to do it some more. It would have been a lot easier to stand up and move around, but if there were Apaches about, that would be the most foolish thing I could do. Chances were, they already knew where I was hunkered, watching for them, but there was no reason for me to advertise.

I was a good thirty yards out from our main camp and one of the troopers, a private named Cook, was on the opposite side of the narrow arroyo, watching that flank. I could hear the camels moving about to my rear and one of the troopers, probably Sid Jordan, was snoring. It had his tone. There was a strange sort of comfort in those familiar noises. Other than that, the night was silent.

The moonlight on the sand and the sparse, stubby growth that dotted the desert cast strange, meaningless shadows. I'd learned long ago that, if you watched one of those shadows long enough, it would seem to move, or maybe change its shape, so I kept my eyes roving, slowly sweeping my gaze back and forth, while I chewed the side of my tongue more out of nervousness than a need to keep awake. If there should be any actual movement out there, I would see it, but the desert I watched appeared almost as white and empty as the moon, itself.

That didn't mean I wasn't thinking about the plume of signal smoke we'd seen that afternoon. That alone was proof enough there was Indians close by, but whether the smoke had been a signal that involved our caravan was something I couldn't know.

Of course, it could be it was some Indian tribe beside the Apache that'd lit that smoke, though I didn't reckon that was the case. As far as I knew, the other desert tribes—the Yumas, the Mojaves, the Yaquis—weren't much for smoke signals.

The tribes of the Great Plains tended to cover their smoke with blankets and flip it aside, then cover again to send up puffs of smoke that sort of spelled out different messages, but I hadn't thought the Apaches were that educated. A straight plume usually meant a positive or a negative to a question that others wanted answered. Or maybe it was a signal for them to gather at the scene of the fire or some other place that had been laid out before. Two plumes, side by side, could mean something else entirely. But this time, there'd been definite puffs. It was a puzzle.

"It's prob'ly some lost Apache sendin' up smoke so they'll come find him," Able Smith had joked, but that's all it was—a joke that nobody even bothered to consider.

And, sitting there in the shadow of the mesquite, I couldn't keep my thoughts off of Beth O'Roark. Slagle seemed to think there was reason enough to be suspicious of her, but I thought of her as a girl with a lot of spunk and maybe not too many brains. The way she had driven her mount to a froth to catch up with us showed she didn't know much about horseflesh and how to treat it. After it had fallen, if Slagle hadn't shot the animal to put it out of its misery, it would have died there in the desert. If we hadn't been close enough to see her, the girl would have been afoot. She wouldn't have lasted more than a few hours in the glare of heat and sand, unless she could have gotten to the river. And she probably hadn't even known there was one nearby.

But it wasn't her time to die, I decided, like it was for Dan Tuppy and the others when their caravan got itself ambushed. That had a lot to do with a sort of philosophy I'd took from old Archie Teech, the wagon master who'd brought me West with him.

We'd been attacked by Comanches early one morning, but had been able to fight them off with less trouble than maybe we'd really expected. When it was all over, the only ones killed was a pair of twin girls, both of them about twelve. They'd been huddled together under a wagon and the same Comanche war arrow had done for the both of them. The flint arrowhead had gone through the throat of one, then on into the other little girl's brain. We'd buried them both there on the prairie and marked their graves as best we could.

Their folks had grieved hard and kept demanding that God should tell them why it was the little ones that had to die. There was no preacher with our wagon train, so Teech conducted the simple service. When it was over, he tried to comfort the father and the weeping mother, but he hadn't done much of a job of it. He'd offered a reason maybe he understood and believed, but it was a view they didn't care to accept.

"When any person is born," he'd told them there beside the double grave, "the good Lord must decide then what day they're gonna die. It was their time. That's just the way it is. Life and death."

What the old wagon master said only made the mother cry all the harder, while the father fretted about how his girls ought to be buried in regular coffins.

After their ma had dressed the both of them in their Sunday best, we'd wrapped them real careful in clean blankets. That was the best we could do. There wasn't a tree big enough to cut a decent board within a hundred miles and, even if there had been, Arch wasn't going to waste coffin-making time, when all he thought to do was get clear of Comanche country as rapid as possible.

I talked with old Arch some time later about the explaining he'd given for the girls dying in so strange a fashion. He termed it something he called predestination. After I'd pondered it some, it came to make an odd sort of sense, but I didn't full realize it till I'd gotten some older and had a chance to observe. Maybe, I'd finally come to decide, old Arch was some right in his thinking.

Over those years, I'd seen several people die I figured shouldn't have. And I'd seen some others live that, by my calculations, should have been dead. Old Arch's theory just seemed to keep proving itself out in strange sorts of ways.

That didn't mean I didn't know fear. There'd been plenty of times in the years since that Comanche attack, when I'd felt snakes wriggling around in my belly, the terror that was them trying to crawl out through my throat. No one wants to die, I don't reckon, and those times I was most sure it was going to happen, I was saying my prayers to God, not asking him to keep me alive; but just trying to get him to understand I still had some things in life I felt ought to be finished. I sort of left it in His hands, figuring that if this was the day I was meant to die, there wasn't much I could do to stop it happening. It may sound sort of crazy, but there was some sort of comfort just in accepting the fact that my life or what was left of it wasn't really my responsibility. If this was the day I was meant to die, I'd just like some sorta sign.

Once, when maybe I'd drunk a bit too much, I told Sam Slagle about what Archie Teech had told to me all those years back and tried to explain my own thinking to Slagle. The sergeant had reared back on his chair and stared at me like he was wondering if I was for sure serious.

"Well, the next time we run across some Injuns or maybe some Mexican bandits, we'll jus' send you out in front to absorb all them bullets. If it ain't your day, you prob'ly won't even feel 'em," he'd announced.

I'd shook my head at him. "You ain't listenin', Sergeant," I told him. "Thinkin' that way don't mean a man can't get bad hurt. You don't tempt fate, 'cause you still might live with a bullet in your spine, but that don't mean it'd be much of a life."

I'd expected Slagle to josh me about my beliefs later on and I was sorry I'd ever discussed it with him. But he never said a word. In fact, he acted as though the conversation had never happened. If I hadn't known better, I might of figured he was so drunk he didn't recall it, but maybe he just thought everybody's God was his own business. Since he was Irish, I always figured him for a Catholic, but I'd never seen him go near a church, even when we was somewhere we could find one.

I sat there under the thin, cold moon, hugging my carbine between my knees, working to keep my eyes moving back and forth, hoping I wouldn't see anything out of the ordinary and not really expecting to. Still, it paid to be almighty cautious.

They always tell about how Indians won't attack at night, 'cause they're afraid if they die in darkness their spirits will wander through eternity. I'd heard all that, but there still had been some cases of Apache staging night attacks, when they felt certain they couldn't lose. Having that sort of information didn't make me feel near as confident as full ignorance might of.

The big Colt Dragoon pistol lay there beside my hip. I'd unstrapped it off the camel saddle and lugged it up into them rocks with me. The single-shot carbine was good enough for what it was, but it still could fire only one round before having to reload it. The Dragoon carried five rounds and could maybe help out a good deal if you was faced with a horde. I'd left the revolver in its holster to protect it against the sand, but I'd turned back the protective flap so I could grab the big wooden grip without too much fumbling around.

I was watching one particular bush and its shadow, trying to figure what was odd about it, when I heard the crunch of sand behind me. I started to turn, then felt a hand on my shoulder. I thought it was Sergeant Slagle, until she spoke.

"I couldn't sleep," Beth O'Roark whispered near my ear. "Can I sit here with you a while?"

"Sergeant Slagle wouldn't like it."

"Why not? Aren't two sets of eyes better than one?" She didn't wait to be invited, but sort of slid down on the sand beside me, scrunching around into the loose soil to make sitting more comfortable.

"There's that, I reckon." I know for certain that Slagle wouldn't like a sentry having company, but I did welcome her being there. I glanced at her to note she had pulled on that old jacket that was too big for her, but her hair looked as though it had been combed and pushed back over her collar. She hadn't bothered with her boots and sat there, digging her bare toes into the loose sand as though trying to hide them.

"Seen anything out there?" she whispered.

"Yep."

"What?" She almost spoke aloud, then realized it. "What?" she repeated in a whisper.

"Miles an' miles of sand an' a batch of bushes."

She didn't say nothing for a moment and I figured maybe she was mad at me for making her seem a little foolish. Finally, she shook her head.

"I had to be a fool to follow you all like I did."

"Yes, ma'am," I agreed. "It weren't the smartest thing you ever done, I expect."

"I was frantic, Jeff. No one would tell me anything."

I nodded, catching the glint of her eyes in the moonlight. "I can understand that."

"Have you ever been frightened that way? Fearful of what you don't know?"

I thought about it some, then nodded. "Reckon I have."

There'd been other times like this, when we was certain there was Indians close about, but there was no real sign. Just waiting could be worse than having them shooting at you. At least, there was some satisfaction in being able to shoot back. The uneasiness came when you knew there was something out there you ought to be shooting at, but you didn't know who it was or where.

"Are we gonna be all right?" the girl asked. She was trying not to sound frightened, but I reckoned the reason she hadn't been able to sleep was in the fact that she'd suddenly come to realize full well what kind of a spot her foolishness had put her in. It might've seemed simple enough to rent a horse and follow a caravan headed downriver to Yuma, but she hadn't known about the renegades or the Apaches then. She hadn't known how quick the desert can kill.

"I don't know," I told her honestly. "Sergeant Slagle ain't took us into his full confidence, I expect, but near as I can figger, we're bait to draw out them that attacked Tuppy's outfit."

At mention of Dan Tuppy, I felt her stiffen beside me. I took my eyes off the desert and glanced at her. "Sorry."

She hesitated for a moment, then nodded understanding. "No need to be. Either of us being sorry won't bring him back." Her tone was flat and toneless.

"How'd you an' Dan come to meet up?" I wanted to know. "You know him in the Old Country?"

"No. Before he came out here, he was stationed in Virginia. He had some leave and came to Boston to see his sister. She was the cook in a home where I was the maid."

Her answer left me sort of disappointed. I'd seen it all before. I'd tended to think of her as some sort of lady of breeding, if that's the right term. Maybe it'd been her show of stubborn recklessness that led me to believe that way. Instead, she was just another immigrant that'd come to America, thinking to pick up gold out of the streets. Instead, she'd ended up catering to some rich Boston family.

The forts where I'd been stationed always had Irish soldiers and the girls who had married them. Most of them made a few extra pennies doing the laundry for the officers and the sergeants, growing old and wrinkled in the desert sun, while their husbands did the only thing they could to make a living in what they'd both thought would be the Promised Land.

"Then you really didn't know Dan all that well," I ventured, reckoning she'd agreed to marry him so she wouldn't have to be someone's maid for the rest of her life.

"I knew him well enough to marry him!" Her tone was stubborn and angry. "Dan Tuppy cut quite a romantic figure!"

I thought about it. Dan had been older than me by several years and he'd been just another camel jockey, hating every minute of it, from what little I'd observed. But in Boston, with his hair cut, his beard trimmed and a dress uniform, he probably could of presented a dashing figure. Chances are, any of us would have seemed so to Beth or any other Irish lass looking for a way out of the scullery.

"I reckon I never seen that side of him," I whispered, staring at her in what I suppose was a thoughtful manner. "Did you love him?"

"Would I agree to marry a man I didn't love?" She spoke aloud this time, angry at my question. I reached up to cover her mouth with my hand. Somewhere behind us, I heard muttering and movement. Her voice had disturbed one of the troopers.

"Sorry," I apologized. "I'm gettin' into stuff that's not my business." I turned to look back across the desert, sweeping it with my gaze as I had before. Then I looked at her again, whispering.

"Go get the sergeant!"

She looked at me, uncertain as to what I was saying.

"Get him. Now!" I ordered in a hissing whisper. As she turned to crawl away, I turned my eyes back to the desert. The bush I'd been watching earlier had seemed different from the rest. Thicker and more dense, solid-looking in its shadow. Now it wasn't there anymore.

Chapter Twelve

Thurlow was not fully awake, but neither was he asleep. He was in that half-world in which he was aware he was no longer dreaming, yet the dream did not end. Instead, it became a fantasy, perhaps even a vision. It had happened to him before and he surrendered to the half-world.

He was in the garden of the plantation back in Louisiana with his grandfather. They were surrounded by the old man's roses, but his grandfather, bent, old, and gnarled, was wearing the garb of a pirate with a gold ring in his ear; a bright scarf covered his head and a cutlass was belted to his waist. The old man did not seem to realize that Thurlow was present or, if he did, he was concentrating too much on his shooting to be interrupted.

The old man was aiming at something in the garden, tracking it with the sights, then pulling the trigger. It wasn't until the third shot that Thurlow noted he was firing a LeMatt revolver like the one carried by Todd Dixon. There was the flash of fire from the muzzle and the gun recoiled visibly in the old man's hand as the shot was fired, but there was no explosive report. Only an eerie, unnatural silence.

In the half-dream, Thurlow spoke to his grandfather, but the old man seemed not to hear. Instead, he appeared angry that he was unable to hit whatever it was he was aiming at with the cumbersome revolver. The sickly, ghost-like figure seemed at the point of tears with his frustration. Thurlow looked through the rose bushes, trying to identify old Jules Dupree's target, but all he could see were the banks of roses in full bloom in a broad variation of hues.

Suddenly, Thurlow realized he had come fully awake, but still he didn't open his eyes. Instead, he lay there, protected by the darkness of his eyelids, troubled at the dream or vision, wondering what it meant. It was almost as though he had not been asleep at all and, instead, it had been a visual prophecy in which his grandfather had been firing the big handgun in an apparently hopeless effort to protect them both from some unknown, invisible danger.

Todd Dixon's obvious, jealous possession of the LeMatt had disturbed Thurlow from the moment he had first seen the bulky revolver and he hadn't known why. Initially, he had pondered whether he had been experiencing his own jealousy that the renegade should possess so rare a firearm, but he had rejected that thought immediately. Knowing the inventor as he did, he could have had one of the LeMatt revolvers for his own had he really felt the need for it. Actually, he had felt the gun was far too heavy and unwieldy for practical use, even with the underslung barrel that afforded one a single load of heavy buckshot at the shooter's convenience.

Of the initial run of LeMatts manufactured in France, less than five hundred of the guns had been delivered to

Dr. LeMatt and about two thousand guns had been brought into New Orleans. These had quickly been purchased, mostly by high-ranking Confederate officers, as personal sidearms. All of the revolvers in this shipment had been .42 caliber, with the bore of the shotgun barrel—which gave the gun its nickname as the Grape Shot Revolver—measuring .69 caliber. The rifled barrel had been six-and-a-half inches in length, the underslung shotgun barrel measuring five inches.

One of the first things he had noted about Todd Dixon's gun, though, was that the rifled barrel had been cut to the same length as the larger bore buckshot barrel, then the front sight resoldered in properly aligned position. The soldering had not been an expert job and looked as though the work had been done by a blacksmith or some other metal craftsman with less skill than a gunsmith. It was possible someone had chopped the length of the upper barrel to reduce the weight or perhaps to make the gun easier to fit into a holster. Before Thurlow had left New Orleans, there had even been talk of producing a Baby LeMatt, which would be much smaller in size than the original and which would fire a .32 caliber ball. In fact, rumor had been that the Confederate government had ordered two thousand of these guns, with the hope of eventually getting them smuggled through the Union blockade.

Since he knew that most of the original shipment had been purchased by Confederate officers, Thurlow wondered now whether Dixon might well have killed one of them to get the gun. Such questions, even the answers, were pointless, the young lieutenant realized. They had nothing to do with what was happening.

Russell Thurlow felt that Rinker, in spite of his efficient killer ways, had some strange feeling of loyalty for the South. Yet, the officer had come to accept the likelihood that were he to face Todd Dixon and accuse him of murdering a Confederate officer to get possession of the LeMatt revolver, Rinker would do nothing. He probably would be interested, true, but that interest would be more concerned with how soon Dixon would gun down the officer rather than making any move to keep the renegade leader from murdering a fellow Southerner.

In considering whether he might have an ally in Jim Rinker, the young Confederate had spent as much time watching him, observing his actions as often as he could, without it appearing an obvious appraisal.

When they had been alone that one time and Rinker had told him about the shipload of Spanish pearls said to be lost somewhere out there in the sand dunes, waiting to be found, Thurlow had felt there was something almost lyrical in the man's way of expressing himself. But when the attack had been made on the camel train, he had seen the cold professionalism with which the frontiersman killed, taking his time and making each shot fatal. That had brought about a whole different feeling. Later, Thurlow had reflected, wondering whether there was not a bit of the poet in the worst of men. He wondered, too, whether that was an original thought, or had he read it somewhere?

There in the protection among the boulders, Rinker had spread his blankets and his pillowing saddle away from the others, seeking some minor privacy, discouraging contact. Each time they had pitched camp, Rinker had done the same. The other renegades sensed that Rinker did not want to associate with them and tended to stay away from him.

On rare occasions, Rinker had joined in their poker games, but those times had been of his own choosing; he was never invited into the games. Also, he never played for more than half an hour and each time, Thurlow had noted, Rinker quit the game to walk away with winnings; no one ever groused that he had quit while ahead.

Even Todd Dixon treated Rinker with an odd sort of deference or, perhaps, Thurlow reflected, it was fear. Dixon also stayed clear of Rinker, except when there was reason to discuss a problem. In those moments, it was almost as though Dixon was willing to share leadership with him. Todd did not openly seek Rinker's advice, but when the old frontiersman made an observation about any decision that faced them, the renegade leader usually followed whatever thoughts the other offered up. That was logical, though. Jim Rinker had spent years traveling the desert wastes. He knew the country, he seemed to know much about the local Indians and their customs, and he appeared to have a more than basic knowledge of military tactics.

Early on, Thurlow had wondered whether the older man, whose face resembled a piece of crumpled leather with its deep tan and sun lines, might have served with the Union Army or some other military organization. He hadn't considered asking, though, knowing Rinker would resent such a question.

While Dixon almost seemed to share leadership of the band at moments, Rinker accepted his orders, silently carrying out whatever duties were assigned, showing neither approval nor disapproval of decisions made. While Todd Dixon tended to bully the others, even swearing at them on occasion, this never had happened to Rinker.

Maybe, the Confederate considered, Jim Rinker was an even more dangerous man than Dixon and the latter realized as much. No need to wake what could amount to a sleeping panther.

Thurlow had watched Dixon become increasingly frustrated by the fact that whoever was leading the camel caravan seemed to expect their moves and had taken steps to avoid a direct confrontation. It seemed to have become a deadly game of cat and mouse. However, he mused, with the increased number of armed Union drovers, there might be a question as to which really was the cat!

Soon after sundown, it had become obvious that the planned ambush of the Union soldiers had gone awry. Thurlow had lain hidden in the sand with the others for hours, waiting for the soldiers and their camels to arrive where Dixon expected them to camp.

Finally, Todd had called in the ambushers and told them to get some rest. At the same time, he had assigned two riders to ride back up the river and find what had happened to the camel force.

Thurlow had no idea how long it had been since the riders had left, but he noted that the moon had covered most of its arc of the sky, moving downward toward the mountains to the west. The moon had been late rising, so it had to be late. The two horsemen should have been back and he wondered whether they might have run into a counter-ambush by those they had been sent to find.

Thurlow suddenly realized he was entertaining the possibility and found it something he favored. When he had come into the Mojave, as ordered, he had hoped they would be able to raid the camel camps near the forts and drive off the animals. But it soon had become obvious that was implausible. When he had suggested it in the beginning, Dixon had laughed at the idea and even Rinker had appeared amused. The base camps invariably were close to the forts and there was no way they could oppose a large garrison force and make off with the camels in the darkness without pursuit soon catching up. The ambush tactics had been Todd Dixon's idea and, as the renegade reminded him bluntly, they did work. The first camels already were on the way to Texas.

But the young lieutenant also realized his mission already had reached an end. The interest of Dixon and the others now was concentrated on the rumored gold shipment. If the Union force was slaughtered as planned and the gold found, they would ride off with these new riches, no longer interested in the hard life and dangers connected with capturing a few ill-tempered beasts.

Thurlow realized the fact that if Dixon got his hands on the gold, he would be killed. In fact, he didn't really understand why he had not been slain before now, unless the renegade was operating on the premise that, if the gold did not exist, they still would have the camels and be able to send them back to Texas for the Confederate bounty.

Either way, his mission, he was certain, had already come to an end. Dixon had been right, when he said they should have scalped the sergeant and his men and left them for the coyotes and the buzzards. It was almost certain now that the Union command realized a Confederate force was in the area and, if a second caravan should be attacked and the animals disappear, the cavalry surely would launch a manhunt in the direction of the border. There would be no way he could convince Dixon and the others to take more risks with the hope of capturing more camels after this.

What had seemed a simple assignment when it had been outlined for him back at Fort Davis had developed into a chain of events that he felt could only end now in a lot of violent deaths. The desert was deadly enough in its own way, but with the war being brought to the sprawling, endless sands, the band of renegades bent on murder and plunder, he was out of his element and realized that he was not prepared for the kind of violence he had experienced in the slaying of the Yankee sergeant and his men. He had been raised in a protected environment, enjoying the life and privileges of a young gentleman until he had enlisted in the Army of the Confederacy. And he had seen no actual military battles. Instead, he had been trained for this single, near senseless mission.

Never before in his life had Russell Thurlow given any great thought to dying, but huddled there in the sand, he realized how mortal and insignificant he was and he wondered whether that simple realization was, in itself, a kind of fear. Realization that your dying would not bring the world to an end. Only your own, particular part of the world.

Thoughts of the strange dream crowded through his mind, scenes and recollections jumbled with each other. Eyes still closed, Thurlow lay with his head on his saddle, trying to recall each part of the sequence. He wondered now whether it really had been a dream or whether his grandfather had come to him as a ghost to warn him and, perhaps, to suggest a way of escape.

There were those, Thurlow realized, who would ridicule his idea that it might have been a ghost, but he had been raised on the plantation and, playing with the young darkies as a child, he had come to recognize their superstitions, even believing in some.

A black slave child named Amos had been his special playmate in those days, since they had been born within hours of each other. And it had been Amos who had sneaked him through the jungle-like growth flanking the bayou one night to spy on a voodoo ceremony. Amos had taken him along under protest and had made him promise never to tell a soul. The Negro child was certain that, if his elders learned what he had done, he would be struck dead by voodoo magic.

The young Russell had been at great effort over the years to put out of his mind the things he had seen that night. At one point, an old woman, obviously a witch, had bitten off the head of a rooster, then had sprayed the assembled folk with blood from the flopping corpse. He had almost vomited. But he had come to believe there were matters beyond his own understanding and that of other whites. Those matters, he acknowledged, had to do with the possibility of another, darker world, one of sinister magic, demons, and horrors. Perhaps it was hell itself. That was the chief reason he could not discount the suspicion that his grandfather had come to warn him.

But if the old pirate had offered him a plan of escape from Todd Dixon and the situation in which he was trapped, he had not been able to winnow it out.

The old man had been dressed in his pirate garb, appearing a bit ludicrous in his advanced age, but the officer wondered whether that dress might have been significant. He remembered the illness that finally had taken the old man, a fever that the doctor had not been able to identify nor treat. Jules Dupree had simply wasted away, angry at the way he was dying. He had been out of his head toward the last and had frequently cried out in the night, seeming to fight one of the pirate battles that ultimately had made him a rich man.

Lying there in the darkness, Thurlow wondered whether, in his dying, the old man had come to realize he would rather have been killed suddenly in one of those battles, sided by Jean Lafitte, than wasting away in a bed, dying a little each day.

And in pondering that possibility, Thurlow wondered whether, in his dream, the old pirate had not been in his rose garden, firing the revolver at Death, unable to hit it. Or perhaps the old man had come to offer him an example, to show his grandson how to die with dignity.

Another possibility had occurred to Thurlow and he gave it more thought, as he allowed his eyes to open enough that he could see across the clearing. The renegades were scattered about, most of them tossing beneath their saddle blankets in restless sleep. Todd Dixon lay no more than a dozen yards from him and, against the night grayness of the sand that had drifted into the hollow in the rocks, he could make out the renegade's squat figure.

Thurlow's revolver lay in its holster only a few inches from his hand. He had thought once before of simply sitting up, leveling the gun, and firing at Dixon until the revolver was empty. The suddenness of the attack might catch the others by surprise and he could tell them he was now in command and that they would take his orders.

But that was another of those plans that sounded too easy. He realized that, the moment a shot sounded, all of the men in the hollow would have guns in their hands and would be firing. Seeing the muzzle flashes from his revolver, most would be firing at him. Too, he had noted earlier that Todd Dixon slept with the LeMatt in his hand, and he never was certain when Dixon was asleep or simply pretending to be. If the renegade was looking for the chance to kill him, leveling a gun in Dixon's direction would be reason enough. Somehow, though, Thurlow knew Dixon was not ready for him to die just yet. The outlaw had a reason for wanting to keep him alive awhile longer and the Confederate officer wondered what that reason could be.

Thurlow's considerations were interrupted abruptly by the sound of boots crunching in the sand and he saw the shadowy figure of one of the night sentries outlined against the stars, as the man glided past to squat beside Dixon's figure.

"Todd," the man half-whispered. "They're comin' in. Both of 'em."

Dixon sat up abruptly and, by thc thin moonlight, Thurlow could see that he was wide awake, the big revolver clutched in his fist. The younger man shuddered, realizing Dixon might even have been aware of his thoughts and had been lying there, waiting for him to make a move.

The two scouts rode into the shallow arroyo, pulling their horses up, as Todd Dixon crossed to them.

"What'd you find?" the renegade demanded loudly, wanting the rest of the camp awake and listening.

"We found 'em," one rider said wearily. "T'weren't easy, though. They took them damned camels into the river an' we had to look up an' downstream, till we found where they came out.

"They're six, seven miles up th' river in a cut sorta like this. Hid in the rocks. There's Injun sign out there, too. Apaches must be lookin' for 'em."

Rinker had risen from his blankets and had moved closer to listen.

"It could be a trap," he cautioned sagely. "They may be waitin' for us with the whole Yankee cavalry."

"Could be," Todd Dixon agreed, pondering the idea for a long moment. Then he made up his mind. "But we ain't gonna know 'less we go look. And we'll never get that gold, if we don't."

Crawling out of his blankets, Russell Thurlow felt a sudden bouyancy, a feeling of excitement. He was almost glad he hadn't taken the shot at Dixon. And he wondered for an instant whether what he was really feeling was raw, undistilled fear.

Chapter Thirteen

"Get Slagle," I whispered hoarsely to the girl. "Quick!" She stared at me, puzzled, not understanding, and I turned to shove the heel of my hand hard against her shoulder. It wasn't meant to be gentle. I wanted her to move. "There's something out there!"

It was easier than explaining that something wasn't out there that should have been. "Keep low. Hurry!" I ordered.

She didn't move for a moment. Instead, she turned her head to stare into the desert, trying to see whatever it was that had upset me. Then she sort of half rolled onto her front side and began to scuttle on hands and knees in the direction where she knew our sergeant was bedded down.

I kept watching, trying to catch some hint of movement, but there was none. Just the bush that should have been there betwixt two others and wasn't. I had the rifle ready for whatever was to come, when I heard Slagle skittering in the sand behind me, then a hand gripped hard on my upper arm.

"What'd you see?" he wanted to know, his whisper

sharp. His eyes also were sweeping the moon-grayed sand that spread to the horizon in front of us. I shook my head.

"There's two yuccas out there 'bout three hundert yards," I told him. "There was three of 'em a bit ago."

"You didn't see no movement?"

"Nothin'. It just ain't where it was."

I expected Slagle to tongue lash me some about the girl being up there with me, but he made no mention. Instead, he hunkered down on his knees at my flank and took to looking, slow and searching. The moon was starting to lower and the shadows was a lot longer than they'd been when I'd took the watch, but I'd given that consideration, too. Sergeant Slagle had the same idea I'd already rejected.

"Them shadows've changed some," he muttered beneath his breath. "Moon's almost down."

I shook my head, although he wasn't watching me. His eyes still swept the desert.

"Moon's got nothin' do with it. There was three bushes. Now there ain't," I insisted, still in a whisper.

He thought about it, still watching, scowling, as I could see out of the corner of my eye. "If there was somethin' out there, it's gone now," he stated. "An' it weren't no white man. You'd sure not let some Johnny Reb get this close without spottin' him."

I reckoned that for some sort of compliment, but I didn't much care for the alternative. He meant I'd been watchin' an Indian. An Apache, no doubt. They were almighty good at being a part of the landscape.

"If he was out there that long, he prob'ly knows we're here," I ventured. I was hoping Slagle would have some logical reason not to agree with me. I also knew that wasn't likely.

"He knows by now how many of us there are and

prob'ly right where each of is bedded down," Slagle agreed grimly. He turned to glance at me. "Stick here for now. Keep watchin' hard an' I'll send Smith up to relieve you."

"The girl. Beth," I started. I was going to make an excuse for her being with me, but Slagle interrupted.

"I told her to get some sleep." I'd offered him the full chance to tell me I'd been derelict in my duty, allowing the girl to sit there with me while I was on guard, but that was all he said before he backed away on his hands and knees, then turned to scuttle off.

The sun and the moon, I've noted, both are hurriers when it gets close to the end of their watch. I don't know how many folks have had a chance to observe, but I've seen it many times. After taking their time about getting across the sky, in that last few minutes, both tend to drop like a ball. They disappear in minutes behind a hill, a mountain or just fall below the horizon. Watching, you can see them disappear like a leaky ball sinking in a bucket of water.

That was what I was watching from moment to moment, as I sat there alone, suddenly feeling like I was all by myself in the expanse of the desert. The others were but a few yards back of me, but that feeling of aloneness persisted and gave me an uncomfortable sensation at the back of my neck. I grinned to myself as the thought came that I'd almost welcome the sight of something moving out there in front of me.

Then suddenly the moon was gone and darkness seemed to sweep over the desert. The long shadows were gone, but I could still make out the scattered bulk of the desert growth by starlight. It was that little time between the setting of the moon and dawn that always seemed the darkest and the coldest to me. Maybe it's supposed to be that way.

There was the sound of movement behind me and Able Smith crawled up beside me, settling his haunches in the sand, switching his buttocks about till he was comfortable. He'd been soldiering a lot longer than most of us, though I'd noted others like him. Their thinking seemed to be that, if they stood a high chance of dying, they might as well do their best to be comfortable while they're waiting for it to come about.

With the disappearance of the moon, a breeze had sprung up. I had noticed when it first started, but it seemed to be growing stronger. I looked out across the desert and saw that the desert growth was appearing ghostlike as blowing sand began to obscure it.

"I don't like this," Smith complained in a whisper. "Ain't natural for the wind to pick up this way. Not at night." He was right. In the desert, a drying, cutting wind may blow in daytime, but it mostly dies out just after sundown.

"It's to our benefit," I told him. "It'll maybe wipe out whatever tracks we left behind us comin' outta the river."

He grunted and settled his rifle across his knees. Like myself, I noted, he had brought along his Colt Dragoon, still in its leather holster, and had laid it out close to hand.

"Better try'n get some sleep," he advised.

"What time is it?" I wanted to know, glancing at the eastern sky. There was no sign of dawn as yet.

"Dunno exactly. Maybe three o'clock." That meant it still was two hours or so before it would start to show light.

"You ever see Apaches puff smoke like that before?" I asked. It had been bothering me ever since I'd seen it. It didn't make sense to me, at least.

"Huh?" Smith didn't seem too interested. He was eyeing the two yucca plants that Slagle must of told him about.

"The way that smoke was bein' sent up in puffs," I insisted. "T'ain't the way Apaches do."

"A Patch does whatever he damned well wants to do to get results," Able Smith said grimly. "If he needs smoke puffs, then he'd use smoke puffs, even if he has to take off his pants to throw over the fire."

"That's if he has pants," I pointed out, trying to sound humorous.

"On the other hand, it coulda been a Patch that had the hiccups." Able Smith's comment didn't sound a bit funnier than mine there under a dying moon.

"Keep lookin'," I advised, as I turned to half crawl toward the camp. Able Smith offered a grunt of acceptance in my wake. It was like he was accepting my suggestion, but didn't need the likes of me to tell him how to do his soldiering.

When I was off the skyline, I stood up straight and moved to where my blankets were laid out, taking care to skirt the other figures I could make out only as dark lumps against the lighter color of the sand.

I started to sink down on the blanket, then realized I'd had nothing to eat since midday. Quietly, I moved across the protected clearing on my hands and knees, feeling for my saddle and the saddlebags.

I unbuckled one of the bags and felt around inside till I found a round of hardtack, one of the hard biscuits that have been supplied to soldiers probably as long as there have been wars. I unslung my canteen and, after a bite of the tasteless unleavened bread, washed it down.

We'd halted sometime around noon to chew on more of the biscuits, washing them and some beef jerky down with water from our canteens. I was about to offer some of both to Beth, when Sergeant Slagle stepped between us and handed her a couple of rounds of hardtack and some jerky strips. She gnawed on both, showing that she had been hungry all along, but had been too proud to ask for food.

Tonight, it had been more of the same. Slagle hadn't wanted a fire, since he figured that the smoke might show against the moonlit sky or, at least, whoever or whatever was out there might be able to pinpoint our position by the smell. Now it didn't look as though it had made much of a difference.

It was darker here in the protection of the rocks than it had been on the rim above, where the light, what there was of it, tended to reflect off the rolling sands.

In spite of that, I could see that Sergeant Slagle was not in his blankets. With my eyes growing accustomed to the darkness, I could make out that they had been thrown aside hurried like. That must have happened, when I sent Beth to fetch him up to the rim. But where was he now?

The keg containing the gold had been positioned next to his blanket roll, too, and I realized suddenly that it was gone. I felt something that must have been panic, as I looked about the enclave, seeking some sign of Slagle and the gold. All I saw was the circle of snoring bodies, some of them moving restlessly in their sleep.

"Beth!" I hissed across the clearing, then saw her as she sat up, looking in my direction, trying to determine my position. I rose and moved across the sand, dropping to my knees beside her.

"Where's the sergeant?" I didn't mention the keg full of gold, figuring Slagle would know where it was. Her boots stuck out the bottom of her blanket. Somewhere behind my other questions, I wondered why she'd put them on.

"I don't know," she whispered.

"Didn't you see him when he came down?" I was trying to keep my own words down to a whisper, but the panic was beginning to grow. Slagle gone. The gold missing. What could it mean?

"I saw him. He went off that way." She pointed to a low cut between a pair of boulders. Out there somewhere one of Able Smith's men was supposed to be on guard. "He was carrying something. Clutching it to his chest as though it was heavy."

I didn't know what to do. All sorts of thoughts went racing through my mind. I'd been told I would be in command, if anything happened to Sergeant Slagle. Now he was gone, taking the gold with him. That didn't mean he had run off, I told myself. Chances were he was only checking on the other sentries, but if that was what he was about, would he lug the gold with him?

"What's wrong, Jeff? What is it?" Beth had recognized the dread, the sudden uncertainty I was feeling and she grabbed my arm, hanging on. I tried to pull away, not certain what I was supposed to do, but knowing I had to be free to do it.

"I don't know. Somethin', though."

"Dammit, go to sleep!" a gruff voice called from one of the bedrolls. It sounded like Sid Jordan. We had been speaking aloud, I realized. Some of the others were moving restlessly, turning in their blankets. Someone coughed, then went back to snoring.

That was when the scream came out of the night. It was not a high-pitched, terrorized scream. I don't know how to describe it, though I'd heard the same sound before. It was the cry of a man who knows he's dying and is angry that he can't do nothing to stop it.

Chapter Fourteen

The only sounds in the darkness of the desert night were the creak of saddle leather, the occasional clank of an iron bit against a horse's teeth, the soft rattle of sand disturbed by hooves, as the band of renegades rode beside the twisting river in single file.

Todd Dixon had given the order that they ride with at least a dozen yards between their horses, but this had resulted in a back-and-forth accordion effect. At the rear of the column, Lieutenant Thurlow found himself spurring his horse to close the lengthening gap between himself and the rider ahead.

When he had first been told of his mission, Thurlow had asked in an official letter that the band of Texans who lived near Los Angeles be ordered to aid him in his assignment to capture Union-held camels and get them back to Texas. It had seemed logical to him then—and still did—that Texans should be used for Texas work. However, he had been told that what was left of the band of of the Lone Star migrants were being held for a special mission on behalf of the Confederacy.

Most of the former Texans had settled in a village

called El Monte or just The Monte. Some miles east of Los Angeles, it was near the juncture of the San Gabriel River and the Rio Hondo. Before war had been declared, there had been conflict throughout California, Unionists pitted against the Chivalry, as the Southern supporters of slavery were called. The northern areas, including San Francisco, tended to side with the Union supporters because of the great population of New Englanders who had come around the Horn to seek gold or had simply settled in the northern town after service with the whaling ships out of Massachusetts or the Boston merchant fleet.

But Los Angeles, Thurlow knew, was pretty much the opposite, when it came to political sympathies. It had been pro-Southern and pro-slavery long before the war, even before statehood. Albert Sidney Johnson, now second in command to Robert E. Lee, had returned to the South from Los Angeles to fight for the Confederate cause, but many of his relatives still lived in the Spanish adobe village, attempting to maintain low profiles and avoid involvement.

Several times in the past, the El Monte-based Texans had been called upon by Southern sympathizers to show their strength in demonstration against the Union. More than once, the band of a hundred or so hard, trail-seasoned horsemen had ridden into Los Angeles en masse, armed and ready for trouble, when they thought there would be an open insurrection.

These Texans, Thurlow knew from intelligence reports he had scanned concerning friendly forces in California, were allied closely with the Knights of the Golden Circle. This secret organization had been dedicated to winning the West for the Confederacy even before the first shot had been fired at Fort Sumter in the Carolinas, a continent away. The secret group had launched an effort to bring about the seizure of California for the South and had come so close to succeeding that Union military expeditions had been brought in to crush what amounted to unofficial Confederate outposts.

Many of the El Monte Texans, Thurlow was aware, had fled California, crossing the desert in an effort to return to their home state and join the Confederate Army. But a hard-core group still lived in the area, carrying on a secret guerilla campaign against Union garrison forces.

It had been the contention of the Knights of the Golden Circle that, if California and its gold mines could be captured for the Confederacy, this wealth could do much to win the war. Leadership of the secret group also felt Cuba should be wrested from Spain by the Rebel forces and made a Confederate state. Their belief was that, if the South held Cuba, the pressure of the Union naval blockade on southern ports would be eased and it would be much easier to import guns and ammunition from the European countries willing to sell both to the Confederacy for hard cash.

Whatever the reasoning, Thurlow's official request that the El Monte-based Texans be assigned to his cause had been refused. It may have been, he had considered, that the force was simply considered more valuable in harassing the Union garrisons in occasional guerrilla actions, causing the Yankees to maintain a strong military presence in the Los Angeles area, a contingent that could not be moved east to the fighting zone and thus was neutralized.

Instead, the young officer had been directed to Dixon and his band. Slumped in his saddle, riding on a loose rein to allow his horse simply to follow the rider ahead of him, Thurlow again could taste the bile of his continuing bitterness. He had been saddled with a bunch of worthless, undisciplined outcasts who cared far less about the success of the Confederate cause than they did about filling their saddlebags with Yankee gold! They were not soldiers. They were free-booters. Pirates!

There in the night, that flashing thought brought an instant comparison between Todd Dixon and his own grandfather, old Jules Dupree. Thurlow straightened in his saddle, trying to drive away the haunting, unpleasant thought, but it refused to go. Todd Dixon was a pirate just as his grandfather had been, taking what he wanted, killing to get it. And the others were the same.

The young lieutenant could not put down the chuckle from deep in his throat at the idea of an aged, weakened Todd Dixon puttering in his own rose garden, enjoying his wealth while all of the town thought of him as a gentleman, not aware of where his wealth had come from. Thurlow wanted to consider such a possibility as ridiculous, yet his own grandfather had achieved that end. Why not Dixon, once the war was ended, if he had collected enough loot? Russell Thurlow felt a vague sense of disloyalty at comparing Dixon to his own grandfather and tried again to drive the thoughts from his mind.

With a sudden bunching of horses ahead, the young Confederate jerked his head up, straightening once again in his saddle. Dixon, in the lead, had his hand up in signal for a halt. Slowly, the horseman rode forward to gather about the renegade leader, as he dismounted and handed his horse's reins to one of the others.

"We're close," Dixon hissed in a loud whisper. "Me an' Woodman'll sneak a look at the layout. Stay here an' be ready to move out on foot, when we get back."

Thurlow again felt the boiling of resentment that tightened his stomach. Dixon should have asked him to go along for the look at the Yankee encampment. But, he had to acknowledge, Woodman, a skinny, round-shouldered rider with a scraggly beard, was one of the trackers who had been sent out to find where the camel troops were holed up. Woodman dismounted and, stretching for a moment from the long ride, settled his gunbelt on his hips.

Still resentful, Thurlow watched as Dixon turned to plod through the sand, disappearing behing a dune. Woodman, holding the carbine across his chest, followed a dozen yards behind. Grudgingly, Thurlow admitted that the two were showing some basic knowledge of tactics, taking care not to bunch up as a target.

"Stand close to your horses," Rinker ordered, swinging down from his battered saddle. "If one raises his head like he's gonna whinny, squeeze down on his nostrils. We don't need to tell 'em we're comin'."

Thurlow dismounted like the others and dutifully stood at his horse's head. He draped a rein through the crook of his elbow, then lifted his canteen from the saddle and unscrewed the cap.

The water was warm and tasted vaguely of salt, evidence of the alkali that was heavy in the river, when the water level was down. The officer rinsed his mouth, spitting it into the sand, then took a long drink. In the near darkness, he saw Rinker glance at him as though disapproving. Nothing had been said, Thurlow had noted, but Rinker had automatically assumed command, when Dixon slipped away.

Attempting to act unconcerned, the lieutenant slung the canteen on his saddle and walked toward Rinker, leading his horse.

"What's the plan?" he whispered, halting beside the older man. Rinker cast him a judging glance and shook his head.

"Don't know. Depends, I reckon, on what Todd an' Woodman see up there." He glanced about, scowling. "I don't like it, though. The wind's comin' up. An' it don't blow out here at night less'n there's reason."

"Reason?" Thurlow didn't understand and Rinker's shrug of reply was hardly a satisfactory answer for a commanding officer.

"Reason?" Thurlow repeated, deserting his whisper and speaking in a low, hard tone, making it obvious he expected an explanation.

Again there was a shrug. "Sandstorm, maybe. That could be why we ain't seen no 'Paches. If there's a storm comin', they ain't gonna be out in it. They know better."

Thurlow glanced about uncomfortably. Some of the other riders still sat in their saddles. Others had dismounted and were squatted on the ground Mexican-style. One man was starting to roll a cigarette.

"No smokin'!" Rinker hissed at the man. "Want 'em to smell it on the wind?"

The rider looked up at Rinker, hesitating for a moment as though to argue. Then he nodded and shook the tobacco out of the thin paper, allowing it to drift onto the sand, blowing away, strands separating on the wind.

There really wasn't a wind though, Thurlow noted. It was more of a breeze that seemed to be increasing in strength so slowly that it was hardly noticeable. Yet the sand, like the strands of tobacco, was beginning to move, scudding close to the ground to pile up in little rills, rather than drifting.

"It's a good thing we picked up their trail before the wind covered their tracks," Thurlow ventured. "We'd never have found them."

Rinker didn't reply. Instead, he was tense, staring into the darkness in the direction Dixon and Woodman had taken. Thurlow didn't know how long the two had been gone, but it did seem they should have been back by now.

Then came a single long, anguished cry that seemed to cut through the night, laying it open like a bad wound. That was all. A single scream.

The other riders suddenly were on their feet, staring into the darkness, disturbed by what they had heard, if not openly fearful. Thurlow felt the hair at the back of his neck tingling. Was this the feeling of fear?

"What was that?" The worst fear, he realized, always was of the unknown. His voice sounded half strangled in his own ears.

"That was a man dyin'." Rinker muttered the words as though to himself.

And as he suddenly understood that single cry of finality, Russell Thurlow found himself praying the dead man was Todd Dixon.

Chapter Fifteen

There was only the one scream that came out of the night, but I heard the girl gasp beside me. When I turned, she had her mouth open like she was about to turn loose with a scream of her own. I clamped my open hand over her lips. It was fast, almost like a slap in the mouth, and she grunted with pain.

"Sorry. Just keep quiet!" I hissed at her. I still had her mouth covered.

We weren't the only ones who had heard the death cry. Sid Jordan was sitting up in his blankets, looking around, owl-like. He had his revolver in his hand. Others were coming awake, too.

"Where's Slagle?" Jordan called in a low voice. "An' Smith?"

"Smith's on guard. Slagle's somewhere out in the sand," I told him. I was on my knees then, half rising and moving in the direction Beth had pointed. The direction Slagle had gone.

"Keep it quiet!" I hissed the order, pausing to glance back over my shoulder at Sid Jordan. "And watch close. There's Injuns out there!" Jordan was struggling up out of his blankets, as were the others, when I moved over the top of a low sand dune and around an outcropping of rocks.

Out of sight of the others, I dropped onto my belly. I had my own Dragoon in hand and realized suddenly that I'd left the rifle back there beside my blankets. I wished I had it, although the revolver was certain to be handier out there in the night. It's just that I knew I shot better with a long gun.

Earlier, the desert had been bathed in light from the moon, but when it had gone down, a blackness had come to shadow the sand. Stars were bright overhead, but they didn't furnish that much light. Shadows looked blacker than they were, if that makes sense, and I found myself peering into their depths, expecting to see Indians. There was nothing. And the only sound was my own breathing, harsh and raspy, in the silence.

The wind was rising and the sand was beginning to blow, staying low along the ground. Usually, the nights were perfectly still and even the slightest sound could be heard a long way off.

Lying there, my Colt Dragoon stuck out in front of me, I turned my ear away from the wind, concentrating, holding my breath for as long as I could. Then I heard a sort of grating sound, as though someone was walking on one of the dunes. The sound, though, wasn't measured like footsteps. And whatever it was, couldn't be far off.

I took a long breath, after exhaling the spent air in my lungs, and pushed myself up on my haunches. Stooped over, holding the gun in one hand and using the other as a balance each time I took a step like a fast-moving ape, I moved toward the sound. It was on the other side of another outcropping of black rock that stuck up above the sands.

Again, I stopped long enough to peer into the shadows

of the big boulder, but there was nothing there. I recognized I was scared; I could taste the copper metal of fear in my mouth, but I had to know what was going on. If anything had happened to Sam Slagle, that'd put me in charge. Hell, I thought, irritated, maybe I was already in charge!

I edged around the rock and saw Slagle. He was on his knees, his hands held close together and palms outward, using them as a makeshift scoop shovel to cover a large, dark figure.

"Sam!" I hissed. He whirled, throwing himself flat on the ground. His Colt Dragoon suddenly was pointed at me.

"Sam! It's Wagner!"

He lowered the gun and I scuttled across the sand to where he lay. Most of the Indian already was covered with sand. Slagle shoved the Dragoon into his belt and began to scoop more sand over the body. I couldn't see enough of the corpse in the darkness to tell what kind of Indian it was. Kneeling beside the sergeant, I began to scoop with my doubled hands the same as Slagle, until the body was totally hidden.

We rocked back on our heels, surveying the mound.

"Apache?" I asked, whispering.

Slagle nodded. "Musta been scoutin' by himself or we'd be up to our necks in Injuns by now. The rest can't be far off. They're after us, I reckon."

He rose and began to move along the side of the dune, eyes on the sand. I followed, taking a moment to realize he was following the depressions that were the Indian's footprints.

"Hell!" I muttered in protest. "We don't need to find 'em. They'll get to us soon enough."

"We gotta find his horse," Slagle announced. I didn't understand what he had in mind, but it didn't seem like the time to ask questions. I followed along behind him, noting that the blowing sand, still close to the ground, was beginning to fill the Apache's tracks.

Until then, I'd forgotten about the missing keg. I thought to ask about it, but decided against it. Slagle sure hadn't had it, when I'd found him. I couldn't help pondering if he'd buried it with the dead Indian.

We found a skinny paint tied to a bit of greasewood in a depression between two of the dunes. The horse snorted when he winded us and backed away, trying to pull loose. He'd probably never seen a white man before. Not a live one, at least. I stood back, while Slagle edged up to the horse, crooning to it, and untied it. He looped the war bridle over its head and slowly turned it away from us, until it was facing out into the desert.

He gave the paint a smack with the flat of his hand across the rump and the horse trotted off, the war bridle, little more than a piece of rope tied around the horse's neck and half-hitched through its mouth, swinging loosely. The horse didn't look back at all and disappeared over the top of a dune, still at a trot.

"Why?" I asked then, still whispering.

"If they'd found his horse close in, they'd know their scout was around somewhere near. If they find it a couple miles off an' the tracks've blown in, we might gain a little time."

"That Injun ain't gonna stay buried long," I advised. "Coyotes are certain to dig him up."

"Maybe not tonight." Slagle turned away and headed back to our camp. "I reckon he must've been the Injun you seen out there."

"If he was, he circled the camp," I protested. "I seen him on the other side."

Still walking, Slagle nodded. "That's why I think he

was a scout. He was learnin' all about us before he went back to tell the rest what he'd found."

I considered for a moment before I asked, "How'd he die?"

"He sneaked up on me with a knife, but I knew he was there. When he dived for me, I rolled over and twisted his arm. It was the knife under his own weight that killed him."

"Just like that?" It had been the Indian that had screamed.

"Well, I had to bash his head with a rock," Slagle admitted. "Didn't want him screamin' some more."

We plodded on for a few more yards, getting close to where someone on guard at the camp should spot us. I hoped they'd challenged us instead of just shooting. But I was thinking hard about something else.

"You bury the gold with the Injun?" I asked.

Slagle halted in his tracks and turned. He stared at me for a long moment, scowling. Finally, he shook his head. "No. Not with the Indian."

"But why?" I wanted to know, figuring he didn't want the Indians to get it. "Apaches don't care about gold."

"They do, if it'll buy 'em guns." That's what Sam Slagle insisted, but I was pretty certain that wasn't his reason for hiding the keg. He was thinking of Tuppy and the camel train that had been murdered, their camels run off. That hadn't been Apaches.

"You think there's someone else after us an' gettin' close, Sam?" His face was in shadow and I couldn't see his features, as I waited for an answer. He hesitated for a moment, then shook his head.

"I don't know."

"What about them strange smoke signals? They didn't look like no Injun smoke I ever seen. Think they could've been signals to some renegades?"

Slagle hesitated again, as though he was wondering just how much he ought to tell me. Finally he shook his head. "I don't know that, neither."

He turned and moved on toward the camp. As we crept past the outcropping of rocks, I wondered why we hadn't been challenged by one of our sentries. Then, as we entered the clearing where we'd camped, I knew why.

"Put your guns down real slow!" the man said. "You might not die right off that way!"

He was partly in shadow, but I could see that he was standing there with an arm around Beth's waist and he held a funny-looking gun, its muzzle pressed up against her temple.

Chapter Sixteen

Russell Thurlow glanced around him. Those gathered in a depression on his flank a dozen yards away were moving restlessly, reflecting their nervousness at hearing the scream. It always is the things you can't see that are the worst, the most fearful, he reminded himself.

Nonetheless, the officer could feel the tightness of fear in his own throat, the empty, nauseated feeling in the pit of his stomach, as he wondered what was happening out there in the darkness. Dixon had taken the one called Woodman with him. There were two of them. Someone might have been able to bushwhack one or the other, but whichever one was left surely would have gotten off a shot.

Turning his head, Thurlow's eyes settled on Rinker. The desert veteran was crouched beside a scrubby bush, his head turned so one ear was directed to the area where Dixon had thought the Yankee soldiers were holed up. Thurlow listened, too, holding his breath, but there was nothing. Just the heavy, burdensome silence.

Turning to glance at Rinker again, he was aware that the other was well removed from the rest of the renegade band. He had settled in beside the desert bush deliberately so the thin foliage would break up the hulk of his outline, offering some degree of camouflage.

Rinker, Thurlow thought with a touch of bitterness, was the only one out of the whole outfit, Dixon included, who really knew the desert, who recognized its dangers and took his own precautions to avoid them. The others were bunched together with their horses, creating a huge blob of blackness that loomed in the night.

Rinker had tied his own mount to another stunted growth twenty or so yards to his rear. A horse made a large target in the darkness, Thurlow realized, and wished he had thought to do the same.

But Thurlow also recognized the herd instinct that affected the others. If they stayed clumped together, that meant strength in their minds. Rinker, on the other hand, was well able to take care of himself. He'd probably consider the others a burden he didn't need, when the chips were really down, the officer decided. And what would Rinker think about him?

"I don't like it." Rinker shook his head in frustration as he muttered the words. Thurlow, several yards distant, kneeling beneath his horse's arching neck, wondered whether the man was talking to him or to himself.

"What don't you like?" the officer whispered.

Rinker, glanced at him, offered a vague wave that took in all of the desert around them. "The wind's died down again."

"That's natural. It doesn't blow that much at night," the officer said softly. "It's not supposed to blow, is it?"

"It don't usually blow ever at night. When it does, it means somethin'. Trouble mostly."

Thurlow realized his own voice suddenly had grown louder. Several of the shadows outlined against the dune had turned to look in his direction. He couldn't see them clearly, but the movement of their bodies told him that their fears now were being translated as anger. Clutching the reins, Thurlow scuttled through the sand, dragging his horse closer to where Rinker was sitting, his knees drawn up. The desert man turned to glance at him, then up at the horse that now seemed to tower over both of them. There was disapproval in the stiffness of Rinker's back, as he turned back to survey the desert, although Thurlow was unable to see his eyes in the shadow of his hat brim.

"That scream. You think it was Dixon or Woodman?"

Rinker hesitated, then shook his head. "Neither."

"If one of them'd got caught, the other would have started shooting." Thurlow put his earlier thoughts into words, trying to sound positive.

"That's the way I figger it, too, Lootenant."

Thurlow was surprised at the other man's use of his rank. The surprise was in the fact that at least one member of the band of outlaws still was willing to show some respect for his commission. The officer pondered, recalling his earlier suspicion that Rinker had served in uniform. In someone's army. Somewhere.

"I wish to hell they'd get back," Thurlow muttered, shifting his knees in the sand and straightening his body to look about. All he could see was the dim outline of the desert dunes in the darkness.

"The longer we gotta wait, the longer it is before some of us get killed," Rinker offered. Again, Thurlow was surprised at the man's attitude. Suddenly, he found himself wondering whether Rinker really wanted to be here. And if not, what kept him. In the same instant, he wondered whether he might have found an ally.

The two of them were motionless for several minutes, the only sounds the restlessness of the moving horses, the creak of saddle leather and rattle of bits, as the animals tossed their heads.

Thurlow was trying to remember details of Rinker's

earlier account of the Spanish treasure ship that legend said was buried somewhere in the nearby desert, its load of pearls waiting to be found.

There had been a wistfulness in Rinker's voice, when he told the story, as though finding the ship was one of his goals in life, although he accepted, at the same time, the fact that he never would succeed. There was so much about Rinker that was different from the others.

"Rinker, where are you from?" Thurlow asked suddenly, hissing the words so the others wouldn't hear. He had decided to make the plunge. There was no other way out.

The desert man turned to glance at him casually, then offered a shrug, looking away. "The South. That was a long way back, though."

Thurlow hesitated. "You leave ahead of a posse or what?" he asked finally.

"Somethin' like that." Rinker shook his head, watching the desert. "Don't matter much now."

"But you're still for the South," Thurlow insisted, gesturing in the direction of the others. "They're not. They're all thieves. In this mess for themselves. Just like Todd Dixon!"

Thurlow realized suddenly that he had been talking too loud. He glanced in the direction of the others and saw a ripple effect, almost a snakelike movement, as though a reptile was adjusting its position for a strike. He wasn't certain whether any of them really had heard what he had said or it was his tone that had been disturbing to them.

Rinker didn't look at him. Instead, he seemed to concentrate his gaze on one particular spot in the desert. Thurlow, tensed, stared in the same direction, narrowing his eyes, trying to concentrate. Nothing.

He heaved a sigh, trying to shake off the feeling of dread, and turned to look at Rinker once again.

"When the war's over, we might be able to help you cure whatever your problem is back home." The lieutenant kept his voice low, tone guarded now. In spite of the effort, he heard the words come out as pleading. That is what it is, he realized. Pleading. Rinker still didn't look at him.

"Squarin' things up might be fine for you an' yours, Lootenant, what with your family an' money, but I come from nothin! An' my folks'd like it best if I never come back."

"We all came from nothing, dammit!" Thurlow insisted, suddenly angry. "My own grandfather was a pirate! He sailed with Jean Lafitte. Where do you think our money came from?"

Rinker seemed to be surpressing a chuckle. "That's all the difference right there. You got it. I ain't. No matter where it come from."

In that instant, Russell Thurlow understood the wistfulness he had noted in the desert man's tone, as he had talked about the lost treasure ship. Money could mean respectability; money allowed one to buy it. If it really was true, what was wrong with that? Isn't that what had happened in his own family? His grandfather may have been a pirate, but in the end, the looted money had been what bought respect.

Thurlow started to speak, to pursue his argument, but Rinker swung toward him, rotating his body at the waist in a sudden movement that showed his pent-up anger. His voice was still low, but it was raw with emotion.

"Lootenant, you ever been up North? Up in Yankeeland?"

Surprised, Thurlow hesitated uncertainly before he answered. "Never." He wanted it to sound as though it was the last of his desires, a possibility he would never even consider.

"Well, I have an' I'll tell you now, there ain't no way the Confederacy's gonna win this war. Up North, they got factories, makin' goods. They got Colt, they got Remington, an' Smith an' Wesson to make all the guns they need. We got a couple brothers named Dance down in Texas turnin' out single-action revolvers one at a time in a barn! Wars are won by men with goods, not a batch of Southern gentlemen chargin' the Yankee cannons!"

Thurlow started to protest, but the urgent anger in the other's tone stopped the words in his throat.

"I'm a Southerner, dammit. Sure, I want the South to win, but I'm a realist, too. An' as long as we ain't gonna win, I might as well get somethin' out of it!"

"I said I might be able to help," Thurlow reminded in a harsh whisper.

There was no point in telling Rinker about the guns being bought in Europe. Most of the ships carrying them were being picked off by the Yankee blockade. There weren't enough getting through to replace the guns being lost in battle. Rinker was right. The side with the most supplies won.

"You'd like nothin' better'n to ride out of here an' forget all this," Rinker accused. "I understand that. But you better know that, should you even think too hard about it, I got orders to kill you!"

"Dixon's orders?"

"Dixon," Rinker confirmed. "You're a bad threat to him now."

"You could ride out with me like I said." Thurlow knew he was pleading again, but what other way was there?

"Sure I could. An' how far d'you think we'd get? Todd Dixon'd still get the gold, then he'd run us down an' kill us both before we got clear of this desert.

"Who you gonna turn to for help? The Yankees? You

ain't in uniform, Lootenant. They'll hang you up for a damned Rebel spy!"

That was when the shot sounded, slamming against the night.

Chapter Seventeen

When Slagle and me crept back into the clearing among the rocks, I saw that Able Smith had retreated to the edge of our camp and was staring out at a spot in the surrounding boulders. The other guards also had been pulled in and Smith had situated them behind cover where they were protected, but still could survey the desert—as much of it as they could make out, at least, in the thickness of the night.

Together, hunched to stay below the ring of boulders, the sergeant and I scuttled to where Smith knelt, his carbine balanced on a rock in front of him.

"What's happenin'?" Slagle growled under his breath. Smith seemed to hunch his shoulders in a shrug.

"Don't know eggsackly," he whispered. "There's somethin' out there."

"Injuns?"

Able Smith shook his head. "Don't think so." He hesitated, then cast a quick glance at us. "What happened with you?"

"Apache," Slagle told him. "Prob'ly a scout."

"He's dead'n buried," I put in. "An' we run his horse off, too."

I was supposed to be second in command. It seemed right I should have something to say. Or maybe I just wanted to talk away my own nervousness.

"What'd you see?" Slagle insisted, ignoring me. He kept his voice low, but he had edged up on his haunches so he could see over the rock, where Smith had his carbine balanced.

"Nothin' for certain." Smith's tone was stubborn, though. "Just a shadow. Seemed like a movin' shadow."

Slagle glanced at the sky. There were only the stars that now seemed more distant than they had earlier. "If you seen somethin' movin', it wasn't no shadow."

"That's why I pulled in the guards," Smith told him. "An' I thought I heard somethin' jingle. Maybe like a spur."

"That wouldn't be no Apache," I put in. At least, I had never heard of an Apache wearing spurs. They tended to wear white man's clothing some. They might want to show off their bravery, wearing the tunic of some soldier they'd killed, but I'd never heard of one of them taking a soldier's boots. And they wouldn't be wearing spurs over just their soft moccasins. It didn't seem likely, at least.

Slagle turned to me, scowling. I could just make out his features and recognized how he was giving Smith's report some heavy judging. Looking at me he jerked his head toward the others behind us. Some had gone back to sleep, it seemed, but Sid Jordan was still sitting up in his blankets, rocking back and forth, his carbine balanced across his knees. It was as though he expected howling Apaches to come swarming over the top of the boulders most any instant.

"Wagner, crawl back down there and tell Jordan to wake the others. I want them outta the center of that camp and hid amongst the rocks. Tell 'em to dig in so they'll have cover."

"What about the girl?" I wanted to know.

"You help her. See she gets a good hole dug where she'll be protected."

I was a little surprised at this sudden turn about. Earlier, it seemed he'd considered Beth O'Roark a hindrance we all could do without. But then I'd heard what Apaches did to white women. I could see as how Slagle wouldn't want to be a party to that sort of horror.

I started to scuttle away, but Slagle grabbed me by the shoulder, He nodded to the back side of the clearing where the camels had been bedded down. Looking close, I could see dim movement. One by one, the camels were getting up on their feet.

"Somethin's disturbin' them," he growled. "They prob'ly smell whoever it is."

With my Dragoon revolver still in my hand, I moved down from the rocks and scuttled across the open sand to where Sid Jordan was rocking, seeming ready for whatever might come.

"What was that scream?" he demanded in a whisper, as I settled on my knees beside him.

"Injun. Slagle killed him."

The trooper started to shake his head, as though not in agreement with what his sergeant had done. "He was alone," I added. "Prob'ly scoutin' for us. He's buried under a sand dune."

"Won't take them long t'find him once they reckon he's missin'."

"Rouse the others," I told him. "Tell 'em to git in among the rocks and dig in." I waved in the direction where Slagle and Smith were hunkered. "Smith seen somethin' movin' out there."

"Apaches sure," Jordan said, sounding angry, like he didn't deserve all this trouble.

"Get 'em movin'." I ordered, but my back was already turned on him and I was crab-crawling across the loose sand to where Beth O'Roark was hid in her blankets.

At first, I thought she was asleep and I felt a twinge of what I suppose was jealousy at the thought she could be enjoying her dreams, while the rest of us were panicking over the likelihood something out there was after us. Then I saw the blankets moving, sort of shivering, and I realized she was lying on her stomach, crying, trying her best not to be heard.

"Beth!" I hissed. "Wake up!"

I felt self-conscious about being the one to find her scared and tearful. It didn't seem right I should have to embarrass her, when she was trying hard not to let her fear be seen. At the same time, I couldn't help but appreciate her effort. Fear is catching. It can be passed from one human to another, just like smallpox.

She didn't move and, scrunched down on my knees, I bent over, placing my hand on the blanket where I thought her shoulder ought to be. The way she jerked, I reckoned I was pawing her a lot lower than I'd meant.

"Wake up, lady." I was willing to pretend I didn't know she was crying. I'd always been at a loss whenever any woman cried around me. I didn't know how to handle that sort of thing. Looking back, I reckon helping her with her charade was as much for me as it was for her.

She half turned beneath the blanket, still holding it so I couldn't see her face.

"What is it?" she whispered, trying hard to swallow the tears caught in her throat.

"Slagle wants us to dig in. Build up the sand around

us. We may have a problem." I full knew we had bad trouble, but I didn't want to scare her more than she was. Truth is, I didn't want to scare myself no more than I was, either.

"Come on, lady," I urged, pulling back the blanket and grabbing her by the arm to drag her up to a sitting position.

"No! Don't!" she ordered sharply, voice too loud. I saw then that she had loosened her clothing so she could sleep more comfortable.

"Sorry." I half turned my back. "Get buttoned up. We gotta get some cover goin'."

A moment later, her hand touched my shoulder and I swung back to look at her. She was rolling her blankets into a tight cylinder.

Finished, she shoved them into a chink in the rocks.

"How are we gonna do it?" She wanted to know.

The sand was plenty loose there beneath us. I scooted back a yard or so and began to shovel at it, my hands held together like a scoop. It was the same style Slagle and me had used to cover over the Apache. She hesitated for an instant, and I wondered whether she was worrying about what would happen to her nails or her skin. Most women I'd known—and that wasn't many—worried about that sort of thing.

But Beth heaved herself up to her knees, turning her back toward me, and began to work on the other side of our hole. After a few minutes, I paused, panting. She kept digging, throwing the sand up in a bulwark that would surround us.

"Hold up!" I hissed at her. "Don't wear yourself out."

She was panting, too, open-mouthed, as she sat back on her heels and looked at me. I could see the glint of fear in her eyes, when she glanced toward the positions where other soldiers were digging their protective holes.

Up among the rocks, Able Smith, Sam Slagle and one rifleman were still watching the desert.

"I'm scared," the girl said finally. The words make it sound like she was complaining and wanting me to do something about her fear, but that's not the way it sounded at all. She made the words a simple statement of fact, as though she wanted me to understand should she do something I didn't approve.

"We're all scared," I told her. "We'd be bad-water crazy, if'n we wasn't."

That got me a long look. "But you're a soldier!"

"Soldiers get scared, too, Beth. Some say that makes us better at what we gotta do. Just b'cause we are scared."

"Do you believe that?"

I shook my head, disturbed at the direction the conversation was taking. Like I said, fear can be catching and I wasn't wanting to get caught up in whatever it was she was feeling. I was having too much trouble hanging onto my own calm, making it seem I wasn't too concerned. Just doing my soldiering the way I'd been taught.

"I don't know. Maybe." I glanced to where Slagle and the others were hunkered, dark shadows among the boulders. "It seems to work for them."

I maybe should have told Beth O'Roark I was just as green to this sort of thing as she was. True, I'd been a soldier for a time, but most of it had been a boring sequence of trips up and down the desert with the camels, after I'd finished my early training and come West.

I'd listened a lot to the likes of Sam Slagle and others who'd fought in wars and battled Indians, and I suppose I'd started to copy some of their mannerisms, take on some of the same rough and ready look the veteran horse soldier made a part of his pride. But when it came to a battle, be it Indians, renegades or a squadron of Confederate cavalry, I was lacking pretty much in serious military experience.

But no man wants to admit to a woman, especially one as young and pretty as Beth O'Roark, that he can't stand with the best of them.

"Dig!" I told her.

We went back to the chore and, a few minutes later, I settled back on my heels to survey what we'd accomplished. It was a hole big enough to hide the two of us and, if it came to that, I'd be able to level my carbine or my big dragoon over the top of the heaped-up sand for some steady shooting. It was as good as it was going to get, I figured.

"Get your blanket roll an' settle in here," I ordered the girl, not looking at her, pretending to survey our work. I hesitated before I added, "Get mine, too. We'll be here together."

"Both of us?" I couldn't tell from her voice whether it was a protest or she was just trying to understand how things were to be.

"I reckon I'm corporal in charge of see'n you don't lose your hair or suffer becomin' an Apache bride." My tone was gruff. I wanted to sound that way, because I was feeling some strange stirrings inside of what I reckoned to be my soul.

Like I said before, my experiences with women were pretty much limited back then. I won't lie and say I'd never been with one, but this was the first time I'd ever spent this much time close to what I figured would be called a nice girl were we back East. I really didn't know how to handle the idea of being close and being gruff was the best way of hiding from what was bothering me.

Beth shuddered in the darkness, a vague silhouette against the loose sand walls of our little fortress. She stood up and reached over the edge of our parapet to grab her blankets from the chink in the rocks where she'd stuffed them. She dropped the roll beside me, then leaned a bit farther, grabbing the end of my loose blankets, to snake them into the hole with us.

"He never talked about this sort of thing," Beth O'Roark stated. There was an accusing sound in her voice, as she settled her back against the wall of the hole, facing me. Both of us had been keeping our tones real low, whispering most of the time, but there was an anger in what she had just said.

"Tuppy?" I asked. She had to be talking about him.

"Dan always talked about the good times in the Army," she said. "He told about the parades, the parties, and the regimental dances. He never once talked about hiding in a hole in the ground, waiting to be killed!"

Her voice had started to rise and I figured she was edging on hysteria. I grabbed her quick by the shoulders and shook her hard. She reared back to stare at me, the whites of her eyes wide and wild. Then she started to cry. That was when I grabbed her and pulled her against me, trying to muffle the sound of tears against my shoulder. It wouldn't do for the Apaches to know we had a crying woman in camp. If they didn't already know it, I added to myself.

And I couldn't help feeling there was something ironic in a twisted sort of way about what she'd stated about Dan Tuppy, then about us hiding in a hole, waiting to be killed. Sergeant Tuppy had been killed, then dumped in a hole. The end result didn't seem all that much different.

While the Irish girl sobbed against my shoulder, I could feel the dampness of her tears soaking through my shirt. I raised my head to glance toward the out of focus shadows that were Slagle and the others.

Once, over a few beers, I'd listened to Sam Slagle talk about when he'd been with that Santa Fe trail outfit and the trouble they'd had with Comanches; how they'd stood shoulder to shoulder, firing and reloading during one attack, watching drovers and fellow soldiers fall under the arrows and bullets of the Indians.

"Why do men do that?" I remembered asking him. "Why do they just stand there and wait to die? Why don't they turn an' run?"

Slagle had thought about it for a few moments, glaring into the bottom of his beer mug. "Sometimes they do," he said finally, "but mostly it's pride."

I didn't understand and he could see that. "If one man gives up and runs, others'll prob'ly run, too," he explained carefully. "Officers may tell you it's all that discipline an' recognizin' their duty that makes soldiers stand their ground, but for the most part, it's stubborn pride. Bein' too damned stubborn an' proud to let the man on your flank know you're a coward by seein' you run.

"Besides," he'd added, "when there's Injuns all around, there's not much place to run to!"

Beth's tears had subsided, but she still clung to me, face buried against my shoulder. I wasn't thinking about running, but I was pondering the chances of Beth an' me getting out on our own.

Somewhere behind us, where the camels were tied, one of them belched, the sound rolling out, long and loud and disgusting. Madame Red, I thought. She's always the noisy one. She could get us all killed with her kind of noise, bugling our location.

But I was thinking, too, of the probability of slipping up there among the camels, getting me and Beth up on Madam Red's back and riding off into the night. The fantasy was building in my mind, me figuring how I'd be able to get us past the Apaches and ride up the river, just me and Beth, leaving all this behind.

But I knew I'd never do it. I grinned to myself in the

darkness. Slagle had been right. I'd never want him to think I was a coward. I'd want Beth to think it even less.

"You sonuvabitch!" The scream, vicious with hysterical anger, came from the rocks followed by a shot from a carbine, a long, lingering report that seemed to echo again and again against the nothingness of the desert.

So much for fantasy.

Chapter Eighteen

Russell Thurlow realized he had heard a shout just before the shot had been fired, but he hadn't been able to understand what was said. He recognized the shot as one from a carbine, though neither Todd Dixon or the man with him had taken longarms. The shot had to have been fired by one of the Yankee soldiers. *Or an Indian*, Thurlow added, in his thoughts.

"Hell!" Rinker muttered. "They've done it now!"

Thurlow started to rise, reaching up to gather the bridle reins in his hand. Rinker glanced up at him.

"What're you doin, Lootenant?"

"We'd better get ready to move out." Thurlow tried to force a note of command into his tone, but it wasn't right. His words came out more as a question, seeking agreement. Any hope that the others would abandon this effort died, as the other man shook his head.

"Just stand by," Rinker ordered, but his gaze was directed to where the other renegades were gathered. They were moving about indecisively. One of them was swinging up to the back of his horse.

"Stay put!" Rinker called. His hands were cupped about

his mouth to direct the sound, which he kept low. "An' get offa that horse!"

Thurlow and Rinker both watched as the dark shadows began to still and the unidentified renegade swung out of the saddle. Reluctantly, Thurlow squatted once again beside Rinker.

"What're we going to do?"

Rinker shook his head. "For now, nuthin'. We don't know what's happened. Someone could be shootin' at shadows."

"It does tell us about where they're located," Thurlow suggested.

Then came another shot. But this one was different, sort of a bellowing sound instead of the harsh crack of the carbine.

"Damn!" Rinker snarled under his breath. In the darkness, Thurlow could see the other shaking his head in what appeared to be disgust. The sound, the young officer knew, had been the roar of a shotgun. It had to have come from Dixon's LeMatt revolver that had the shotgun tube centered beneath the rifled barrel.

Thurlow discovered suddenly that he had been holding his breath, waiting for another shot. None came and, after a moment, he exhaled heavily. There was no way of telling what was happening out there.

"That had to be Dixon's handgun," Rinker said, muttering more to himself than to the officer. "He ain't dead, at least."

A true pity, Thurlow thought savagely. He had been tempted for an instant to utter the words aloud, but knew better. Rinker's loyalties, if not his sympathies, lay with Todd Dixon. Speaking his thoughts aloud would only make the desert man more edgy.

Rinker was shaking his head again. "Looks like it's

gonna be a fight. I was hopin' we could surprise 'em and have done with it quick."

"Like with Sergeant Tuppy and the others?" Thurlow demanded. This time he could not remain silent and recognized the pent-up anger in his own tone. "Another slaughter?"

"Things happen in war, Lootenant." Rinker said it softly, as though trying to explain a disappointment to a child. He still stared out across the desert in the direction Dixon and Woodman had gone.

"That wasn't war, Rinker, and we both know it. It was out-and-out murder!" Thurlow was recalling again the quiet efficiency with which the desert man had taken his shots during the ambush. Just a man doing an everyday job of killing. "And this isn't war, either. It hasn't been since Dixon found out about that gold. It's been nothing but a plan for robbery!"

"If we take it, that'll be gold th' Union can't use against us," Rinker argued, tone hard, as though he'd had his say and didn't intend to discuss the matter further. Suddenly he stiffened, raising his head to peer into the darkness. Reactively, Thurlew looked in the same direction. A dark figure, little more than a shadow, was slithering across the sand toward them. Whoever it was seemed to be crawling on his belly. Thurlow heard the hammer come back on the Colt revolver Rinker held in his hand.

The lieutenant's first thought was that the figure was one of the Union soldiers, conducting a reconnaissance of the area. He was tempted to shout a warning, but the cry caught in his throat.

"It's Dixon," Rinker muttered, rising to his full height and allowing his right arm to drop, his revolver muzzle pointing at the ground.

"And he's alone," Thurlow muttered. Woodman was not with him.

Neither said anything until Dixon, apparently seeing Rinker's figure outlined against the dunes and the sky, realized he was on friendly ground. The hulking figure rose and trotted into the protective dunes.

"Where's Woodman?" Rinker demanded, as Dixon stopped, panting, in front of him. The renegade chief jerked a thumb in the direction from which he had come.

"Out there. Dead."

"Your shot?" Rinker asked. Thurlow knew then that Dixon had fired that second shot and why.

"He was gut shot," Dixon hissed. "I couldn't leave him to them blue bellies. He'd talk."

Rinker considered the matter for a moment, then holstered his revolver, seeming to relax, accepting the explanation. Thurlow felt his stomach roll and thought he was going to vomit.

"What'd you learn?" Rinker wanted to know.

"They're no more'n two hundred yards over there." Dixon swung an arm to indicate the direction. "Back in a bunch of rocks where they've got good cover. Me'n Woody circled the whole camp. Seen a pair of 'em buryin' somethin' and checked it after they took off. Thought maybe they'd buried the gold." He paused, waiting for the question.

"What was it?" Thurlow finally asked.

"A dead Injun. Apache scout, I reckon. They run off his horse an' made sure the wind was wipin' out sign.

"We was headed back here, when Woody got careless. One of 'em saw 'im an' cut loose."

"Then they know we're here." Rinker's statement was acceptance of his own opinion. Dixon nodded agreement.

"They know somebody's out here, but they may think it's Injuns," Todd Dixon said. He grimaced and shook his head in disgust. "I wasn't thinkin', when I fired that shot on Woody. Could just as well've used a knife. Then maybe they'd think they was shootin' at a coyote.

"Come on," the renegade leader added. "Let's talk 'bout how we're gonna do it."

Rinker followed Dixon toward the others. The Confederate lieutenant hesitated for a moment, then dropped the reins he'd been clutching, leaving his horse to stand ground-tied.

The others gathered around Dixon. Some fidgeted, wanting to ask about the shooting, wanting to know what had happened to Woodman, but no one spoke up. Instead, they moved restlessly, uncertain as to what was to come next.

"There's as much as a hundret thousand dollars in gold in that camel camp," Dixon told them, "an' we kin get it, if'n we play alla our cards right." He spoke now in a normal tone. With the Yankees a good two hundred yards away, there was little likelihood the sound of his voice would carry that far.

"If they're dug in among the rocks," Thurlow interjected, "we can't just charge them."

Dixon caught him a glance of disgust. "That's right, Lootenant. But we can make 'em think that's what's happenin' an' take advantage."

Todd Dixon's plan was simple enough. Most of the renegades would slip out into the desert and form a skirmish line along the top of the sand dunes overlooking the camel camp. Others would circle around and come in from the opposite direction.

"At a given time, you all start firin' on 'em. They'll start firin' back. That'll give us a chance t'take out 'th sentry on their rear side and come in on them that way."

"Tricky," one of the others muttered, not fully accepting the plan.

"You gotta plan of your own that's worth a hundret

thousand dollars?" Dixon demanded, glaring at the speaker. The man stepped back, shifting his eyes and shuffling about. Dixon glanced about the circle of his followers, seeking any other signs of dissent. Finally, he turned to Rinker.

"Rinker, you pack a pocket watch, don'cha?"

The reply was a nod. Todd Dixon turned to Russell Thurlow. "An' I know the lootenant's got one. What time is it right now?"

The officer dug deep into his jacket pocket to bring forth the bulky heirloom his grandfather had left him. He flipped back the cover on the gold case and angled the watch to look at the dial in the faded light from the stars. The black hands were barely visible against the white face of the timepiece.

"Ten minutes till four," he answered finally, looking up. But Dixon already had turned his attention to Rinker.

"What's yours say?"

Rinker nodded. "A coupla minutes later'n that. Close enough."

Dixon nodded at him. "I want you to take the men, all but one, an' spread 'em along that dune to the west. Give us forty-five minutes to get in proper position, then open fire. Give them blue bellies somethin' to really keep their attention!"

He turned to indicate one of the others. "Clem, you'll stay here with the horses." Then he looked at Russell Thurlow. "Lootenant, you come with me."

Less than five minutes later, the riflemen led by Rinker filed out of the depression between the sand dunes. Dixon had briefed them on the exact location of the sandy elevation, where they were to set up their base of fire. The one called Clem had walked out to gather up the reins of Thurlow's horse and to untie Rinker's mount from the bit of growth, leading both to where the other horses stood.

Dixon had spent several moments reloading the shotgun barrel of his LeMatt revolver and now slung it in the bulky holster, taking his own carbine from its saddle scabbard. He glanced at Thurlow.

"Ready, Lootenant?" He didn't wait for a reply, but moved off across the sand, taking a direction almost opposite that in which Rinker and his band of misfits had gone. Balancing his own carbine in the crook of his arm, Thurlow followed Dixon between the dunes, knowing it would be dawn soon after they reached the edge of the camel camp.

At first, Thurlow wasn't certain Dixon knew where he was headed, but the young officer soon realized the renegade was leading him in a wide circle that should bring them in on the opposite side of the Yankee's rock-protected enclave. They slogged through the deep sand, occasionally crossing an area where the sand had blown free, displaying an expanse of hardpan or bare rock. Dixon was taking care to stay under cover of the dunes, crossing them to be silhouetted against the skyline only when there was no other apparent route.

The deep sand was heavy going and Thurlow was sweaty and panting, when Dixon halted and held up his hand. The two of them stood there, breathing heavily for a moment. Forty yards away, Thurlow could see the dark mass of boulders sticking above the level of the light-colored sand.

"Looks like they've pulled in their outposts," the renegade whispered. "See that notch between them two big rocks?" He pointed and the lieutenant peered over his shoulder to determine the position.

"They had a sentry in there. He's gone now. Just b'yond them rocks is where they got the camels bedded. We kin go in that way an' use the beasts for cover." Dixon glanced at him. "What's th' time?"

Thurlow pulled the watch from his pocket and flipped back the lid once again. He could see the face more plainly now and realized it was growing light.

"Nice watch," Dixon commented and Thurlow couldn't help scowling.

"We have four minutes," he announced, quickly closing the face and pocketing the timepiece.

"When the shootin' starts, we wait about thirty seconds, then we head for that notch. Work in behind 'em an' take 'em."

Thurlow nodded his understanding, checking his carbine to be certain it was in operating order. He had just lowered the gun, satisfied, when the first shot sounded. That had to be from Rinker's saddle gun. An instant later, other rifles began to sound from somewhere in the desert.

"Stay low, so you don't get hit by our own fire!" Dixon advised and started to move toward the notch in the rocks, bending low to the ground, his carbine held across his chest.

For a single instant, Russell Thurlow thought of shooting the renegade in the back, but then his bulk was hidden by rocks. The lieutenant followed, finding Dixon hunkered just inside the ring of boulders.

Climbing toward them, carefully picking his way up the steep rocks, was a Union soldier, clutching his carbine. Apparently someone had decided this area needed protection after all. As a bullet from out in the desert ricocheted off one of the boulders, the camel soldier ducked low, hesitated, then continued to scramble upward. He was almost within Thurlow's reach when Dixon stepped boldly from behind a protective rock and swung the butt of his rifle in a vicious arc that caught the soldier on the jaw. Without a sound, the soldier folded and tumbled to the bottom of the ten-foot rock wall, falling at the feet of one of the camels that were crowded into a corner of the fort-like enclave.

It was growing more light by the second and Thurlow had seen the renegade's cruel grin as he watched the unconscious man tumble backward, landing on his shoulders and back of his head.

Thurlow knew that the man was dead. If the butt stroke hadn't killed him, the manner in which he struck the rock protruding from beneath the sand below certainly would have broken his neck.

Dixon glanced at the lieutenant and jerked his head to indicate the way down. The renegade began to half slide, half clamber down the rocks, until he was hidden among the camels that now were moving about nervously. Only one animal, a huge red-colored creature, seemed unperturbed and continued to munch whatever it held in its mouth.

Dixon, keeping low, worked his way among the animals, Thurlow close behind. As the renegade came near, the red camel turned and tried to bite him, but Dixon twisted nimbly out of the way. Fire was still being exchanged, the carbines echoing across the desert, while closer the answering fire of the Union soldiers sounded. Bullets, striking the rocks above, ricocheted from time to time, whining off into the night. One of the ricochets found a mark and a camel offered a grunt, then what sounded like a sigh of final surrender, as it dropped in its tracks.

That's one we'll never get to Texas, Thurlow thought to himself. But none of these camels were ever going to make it back to Fort Davis.

"Camel down!" a voice cried out. The sound stopped Dixon in his tracks. The voice came from no more than a dozen feet away, just beyond the moving, jostling animals.

Thurlow watched as Dixon moved on, maneuvering slowly between the camels, until he could see from where the warning cry had come. The animals were milling about, stamping their feet and pulling at their halter ropes in an effort to escape the growing danger. The officer had to dodge swinging hindquarters several times as he moved forward to look over the renegade's shoulder.

Two people were in the deep hole that had been scooped out among the rocks. They were well protected and, looking beyond them, in the grayness of dawn, he could see other protective revetments that had been thrown up. Rinker and his men were wasting their ammunition. It was a strong defensive position and only a lucky head shot would be effective.

Then one of the people in the hole closest to them turned and Thurlow felt the stab-like sharpness of surprise. Her hair was long and curly and, even beneath her men's clothing, he could see the swell of her body.

"It's a girl!" he hissed at Dixon, but the renegade was already on the move. He scuttled across the few yards separating the camel herd from the fighting hole and swung his rifle butt again, catching the soldier in the hole a glancing blow. As the soldier dropped, Dixon leaped into the hole, tossing his carbine aside. The LeMatt pistol, suddenly in his hand, was pressed against the girl's temple!

"Stop firin' or I'll kill the girl!" Dixon screamed over the sound of gunfire.

Chapter Nineteen

Huddled there, beside Beth O'Roark, my carbine stuck over the edge of the sand revetment we'd scooped up, I felt pretty worthless. Guilty, even. Everyone else was up on the line, firing at whoever was out there, shooting up our camp. From where I was stuck in that hole, there was no way I could get a shot.

A bullet went over our heads, spattering against the boulders, ricocheting away. Beth already had hold of my arm, but when that bullet screamed off into the night, making an eerie sound like it was something dying, she hung on even tighter, pressing herself up against my shoulder. I could feel her bosom heaving against me and I realized, in spite of all that was happening, that this was no girl. Beth O'Roark was a full woman.

"Nothin' to worry about," I told her. "The one that hits you's the one you ain't gonna hear."

For a fact, I didn't know that was true, but I'd heard some of the old horse soldiers talk about being shot during the Mexican War and most of them didn't even remember being hit. It was like there was blank space in their memories created just to cover the pain and shock,

I reckon. The only reason I'd said that to the girl was to try to make her feel a little less fearful.

"Those aren't Indians out there!" She couldn't help the horror in her tone. "Those are the same people that killed Dan Tuppy!"

I was still watching, trying to figure the direction the fire was coming from by observing where Slagle, Jordan, and Smith were directing their shots. It seemed like it was in the direction where I'd seen the shadow we'd figured had to be the Apache scout.

But, like Beth, I knew these weren't Injuns. I was on the point of agreeing with her, when I heard a shuffling somewhere to the rear at the same time another carbine bullet ricocheted off the boulders behind us. The camels were getting restless, and there was a grunt of what sounded like surprise. I glanced back and saw one of the camels slowly fold at the knees, as it might if it was going to allow someone to get into its saddle. But there was a spreading patch of darkness on its neck and I knew the animal had been hit. The camel slowly rolled over on its side. It kicked once or twice, then was dead. There was no mistaking death, one of the things I'd learned about in my first Indian fight.

"Camel down!" I shouted. I didn't know why I yelled out like that. Maybe I was just wanting to feel I was doing something useful. No one on the firing line bothered to look around. They was too busy shooting.

"What happens if they kill all the camels?" Beth wanted to know, snuggling against my shoulder like she wanted to make herself part of me. "We'll be marooned here."

"Well, we got some water and we got some food," I told her. "An there'll be camel meat, if nothin' else."

I don't know why I said that, neither. I wasn't trying to be cruel. Maybe it was to take her mind off what had come to Sergeant Tuppy. Maybe I was just taking out my anger. She pulled away from me and gagged. I could hear her, even though I didn't look around.

I'd thought by now that the firing would slow down, but it hadn't. There had to be a reason, I figured. The camels were moving around behind us and I started to turn. At the same time, I realized Beth had sensed something, too. She was whirling in the same direction.

"It's a girl!" Someone said behind us, more a loud whisper than a voice. I started to rise, trying to swing my carbine on the vague moving shape that loomed over us. I saw the rifle butt coming at me and tried to duck, but I was too late. There was a flash of red pain, then a lingering gray that turned to black. I knew when my carbine fell out of my hands, but it didn't seem important.

The last thing I remembered was a voice that seemed almost next to my ear, yelling, "Stop firin' or I'll kill the girl!"

My head was throbbing something frightful, when I tried to sit up and I panicked for an instant, thinking I'd been shot. Then I noticed the silence. The shooting had stopped. And my hands were tied behind my back. Blinking my eyes against the pain, I slowly managed to push myself upright in the hole. Beth was gone.

My body must have kept turning after I'd been swiped by the gun stock, because I found I was facing the camels. There was movement behind me and I could hear voices, but they seemed to be a long way off. I shook my head, trying to get what seemed like some sort of plugs out of my ears. It didn't help.

Slowly, I scrunched around in the hole, until I was in position to see over the top of the revetment. My carbine was gone, too, I noted and standing directly in front of me was a man, maybe a year or so older than me. He had strips of latigo in his hands and was tying Beth's hands behind her. She was standing back from the edge of the hole and moved about, fighting against the man's efforts.

"Stand still or I'll have to take painful steps, ma'am," the man said. He was dressed like a Mexican and part of his face was shadowed by the big sombrero he wore. That's when I wondered how long I'd been out, for it was light now. Dawn was turning into morning.

Even without seeing all of his face, I knew the man was no Mexican. He had a Southern accent, smooth and syrup-like, though I could hear the strain in his tones. I sat back against the wall of the hole and tried to get a better look at him, as he finished tying Beth and slowly turned her away from me.

"Sit down there, ma'am," he ordered. "You can rest your back against that rock."

I watched as Beth O'Roark took a couple of faltering steps and slowly sank down in the place he had indicated. Other than having her hair mussed a little, she didn't look none the worse for wear.

My hearing was coming back. When the man had first spoken to her, it had sounded as though he was talking into a milk pail. At the last, though, he started to sound more normal. He turned now to look down at me.

He looked Mexican, with his hat and clothes, but his eyes were a sort of light blue and the dark color of his hide was more from sun than birth. He stared at me.

"You sit tight, Corporal, or you may get killed," he warned. There didn't seem to be any anger or even threat in his voice. He was just offering me an option, as though he figured I'd be smart enough to do what was best for my own future.

He turned and walked off. The way I was hunkered down in the hole, I couldn't see where he went. Trying to ignore the pounding in my temple that threatened to drive me cross-eyed, I got my feet under me and pushed myself up a bit, my back against the side of the hole so I could see over the top of the piled-up sand.

I was surprised. There were only two of them. One was the rebel who'd tied Beth and probably me, while I was still out. The other man, older and heavier, was holding Slagle, Jordan, Smith, and the other troopers under a funny-looking gun that seemed even bigger than the Colt Dragoons we carried. It had a second barrel slung beneath that looked to be bored for shotgun use. I'd never seen nothing like it before and, for just an instant, I wondered whether this was all some sort of bad dream.

But there was nothing dreamlike about the two dead troopers that lay sprawled among the rocks. Whoever had been shooting from our front had killed them. Like the camel I'd seen fall, there was no doubt they were dead. There was an ugliness about the way they were sprawled that was final.

"All right, gentlemen, if you will turn your backs one at a time, I will tie your hands," the one in the Mexican hat said. "Make any move against me and Sergeant Dixon will kill you." He paused to be certain they understood, then nodded at Sid Jordan, who was at the end of the line, glaring at him. "You first."

For just a second, I thought Sid was going to jump him. That was until I heard the hammer thumbed back on that big gun in the other man's hand. Jordan glanced at the gun, then slowly turned his back, bringing his hands together. The man used more latigo, what looked like saddle strings, to tie Sid's hands. He checked his knots, then nodded to the next man. The process went on without incident and I looked away, glancing about for something I could use to cut my own bonds. There was nothing. There wasn't even a rock sticking out of the side of the hole that I could use to rub against the leather to weaken it.

All of our rifles and Colt Dragoons, I noticed, had been gathered up and piled in a little cleft in the rocks a good dozen feet from the nearest trooper. These men, I recognized, were not taking chances.

"Worked better'n I expected," someone said and I glanced back to the lineup. More men were coming over the top of the boulder-strewn rocky crest and I realized what tactics had been used against us. These new animals had laid down a base of fire to keep us occupied while the other two had come at us from the rear. It was a basic military maneuver that had been used since the days of the Rome legions.

One of Able Smith's troops had been guarding the rocks up behind the camels, covering that approach. Now, looking over the other prisoners, I didn't see him. He was probably dead, I realized. These people knew what they were about.

Somewhere down in my stomach there was the feeling of fear and it was growing. I knew Beth had been right. These were the same men who had killed Dan Tuppy and his camel detail. But they were treating us differently. Why hadn't they simply slaughtered us and driven off the camels?

I glanced to where Beth O'Roark was seated, leaning back against the boulder. In the growing light of morning, I could see that she was pale; scared stiff, I figured. She had her eyes closed, as though trying to shut out what was happening. And what was going to happen. I didn't much blame her.

"Now hear me!" The one in the sombrero had edged away so he could see Slagle and his group, as well as keep an eye on Beth and myself. Hands of all of the camel troopers had been tied with the lengths of leather and they'd been made to sit down in their tracks.

"I am Lieutenant Russell Thurlow, Army of the Confederacy, and you are my prisoners," the young man announced, his tone soft and formal. I reckon it was what you'd call the voice of a schooled Southern gentleman, but there was that growing strain behind his words and, from the way he was wrapping and unwrapping a length of latigo around his hands, it was apparent the man was nervous. Bad nervous. Maybe even scared, which didn't make much sense. I was scared, but I had a right to be. He didn't. He was in control.

Sam Slagle was eyeing him, glaring really, looking the Mexican outfit he wore up and down. "In that outfit, you're a damned spy!" The sergeant turned to spit in his direction. One of the renegades took a step forward and slammed a fist against the side of Slagle's head, sending him sprawling onto his shoulders.

"That's enough!" the Confederate lieutenant ordered sharply. Then he glanced about, frowning. He turned to look at the man with the strange-looking revolver. "Where's Rinker, Sergeant Dixon?"

"He'll be along. Said he had to check some matters."

"If he's checkin' for Injuns, he won't see none," Slagle growled. "But be certain they're there, watchin' us. If they didn't know where we are before, all that shootin' told 'em for sure."

"Shut up!" the one called Dixon snarled, swinging the muzzle of the revolver to bear on Slagle's chest. "Where the hell's the gold!"

"That's enough, Sergeant Dixon," the younger man said softly, but he was looking at Sam Slagle. "However, the point has been made. We want the gold."

"What gold?" Slagle growled, lying there on his elbows, looking up at the men who towered over him. "You're talkin' like a man with a paper head!"

"Just give us the gold and we'll ride away," the lieutenant said, trying to sound reasonable, but he was worrying that length of latigo even harder than before. He was mighty young for an officer, I figured, and maybe wasn't all that certain about how he should be handling this situation.

"That the way you talked to Dan Tuppy before you butchered him and his men?" I yelled from where I was sitting. The lieutenant whirled toward me, staring, then waved a hand in my direction.

"Get him over here with the others," he ordered. Dixon looked toward me, then nodded to two of his men. They shambled across the sand and reached down to drag me out of the hole by the shoulders. On my feet, I found I was still dizzy and started to stagger toward where the others were seated. One of the renegades planted a foot in my rump and sent my sprawling in the sand next to Slagle.

"What happened to Sergeant Tuppy and his men has nothing to do with now," the officer insisted. But Slagle wasn't looking at him any more. Instead, he was staring to where the camels were tied up. They had settled down since the firing had stopped. I looked in the same direction and saw a tall, sunburned man working his way between them. He had a rifle in the crook of his arm and just from the way he carried himself, something seemed different about him. The rest of these so-called Confederates were ruffians, scavengers, but there was a sense of confidence about this one; a sureness of what he was doing.

"Hello, Tom," Slagle said softly, as the man strode up and paused to face the lieutenant.

The newcomer turned to stare down at Slagle, then nodded, offering a thin smile of recognition.

"Howdy, Sam. Shoulda known you'd figger in all this somehow."

Chapter Twenty

"You've sure dropped a long way down the social ladder, if this is the kinda friends you favor now," Slagle said easily, smiling up at the man he had called Tom. It was as though the others weren't even there and he was talking to an old friend.

"You know each other?" Thurlow demanded tersely, glancing from one to the other. In spite of his strict demeanor, it was obvious he was surprised and curious.

"You might say that, Lootenant," Rinker answered, still staring down at Slagle. "We soldiered t'gether a long way back."

"You was a blue belly?" Dixon demanded, scowling. The accusing tone of the question didn't seem to bother Rinker. He still eyed Slagle speculatively, as he answered.

"Yep. A real, live Yankee soldier. Th' same as Robert E. Lee. Jeff Davis, too, for all that."

"An' a good soldier he was," Slagle declared. He almost seemed to be enjoying himself. "Till he killed a sergeant. After that, he wasn't Corporal Thomas A. Ringgold anymore. Just plain ol' Tom Ringgold, deserter.

Rinker offered a shrug, almost looking sheepish at recollection of his desertion. "If I'd stuck around for th' court-martial, they'd've hung me."

"That they woulda," Slagle agreed, but his eyes were sweeping the other renegades who were watching. They seemed uncomfortable at the casual familiarity between the two men. "But one can't really kick about a new rope! An' I reckon it was just delayin' th' inevitable. You'll hang sooner'r later with th' resta this rabble."

"You mouthy bastard!" Todd Dixon stepped forward to aim a kick at Slagle's head. The sergeant obviously had been expecting such a move and was able to roll enough that the renegade's heavy boot caught him on the shoulder, but still with enough force to knock him flat on his back.

"Leave 'im be," Todd," Rinker ordered. He had Dixon's shoulder in his grasp, swinging him away with what appeared to be little effort. Dixon turned on Rinker, the odd-looking revolver still in his hands. The lines in the renegade's face were deepened by his rage.

"You a Yankee-lover?" he demanded, the muzzle of the revolver starting to rise. The carbine still lay in the crook of Rinker's arm. His thumb was on the hammer, his finger on the trigger, as he shifted the balance of the longarm until the end of the barrel was almost touching Dixon's chest. The move had seemed casual enough, but there was no one watching who didn't realize it was deliberate.

"I tole you once't not to ever point that gun in my direction," Rinker said mildly. "It could get you dead in a hurry."

"Stop it! Both of you!" Russell Thurlow, brushed aside the carbine muzzle to wedge himself between the two. "This is no time to be fighting each other!"

Dixon hesitated, on the point of elevating the LeMatt, again. Then he blinked and offered a tight nod. "He's right." He was speaking to Rinker rather than the officer. "An' like you said, General Lee was a Yankee once hisself."

He smiled, but there was no humor in the expression, no acceptance. Just an ugly spreading of the lips that Thurlow had come to recognize.

Russell Thurlow was aware that Todd Dixon was playing with him, allowing him to seem to be in command, when all of the renegades know the outlaw leader was running the show. If there was a reason for Dixon taking this approach, however temporary it might be, the young Confederate didn't understand it, but he did feel better, attempting to carry out the duties of an officer instead of playing lackey to the spurious Confederate sergeant. He turned to look down at the prisoners lined up before him, inspecting each carefully. All seemed to have taken Slagle's lead and returned his look with baleful glares that verged on arrogance. Thurlow's eyes rested on the young corporal he had tied earlier, when he'd been unconscious in the hole with the girl.

"What's your name, youngster?"

"Corporal Wagner, sir. An' I'm possibly older'n the lieutenant, sir." The third person usage was formal military recognition of an officer by one of lesser rank.

"An' I don't know nothin' 'bout no gold." Wagner pushed himself up on his elbows, a note of defiance in his young voice that brought a chuckle from Slagle.

"You know anything about torture, Corporal? Chinese torture, for example? Burning slivers under your fingernails. The Chinese can make Apaches and Yaquis look like amateurs."

Surprise showed in the young corporal's face and Russell Thurlow recognized the reason. It would surprise Wagner that a Rebel might know that much about what went on in a place as far away as China. Most of them probably didn't, but his grandfather had been there before he finally had left the sea and settled down. Russell Thurlow had heard much as a child at his knee.

The Confederate was certain that, among the rank and file of the Yankee enlisted troops, the capabilities of the Rebel soldier were considered a joke. Even in the South, there was a feeling that the Army of the Confederacy was made up of a group of spoiled planters who tended to ride into the face of cannon fire with flags flying, caring more about putting personal honor and bravery on display than in winning the war.

But Thurlow also knew the Yankee infantry and cavalry had abandoned that impression early in the war; at least, the ones on the battlefield. Even the scattered war reports that reached the West verified that the Rebs had been winning more than their share of battles, even with their dwindling supplies.

"I don't know nothin' about no gold!" Wagner repeated again, but Thurlow could see the fear that was beginning to grow in the young man's eyes. He looked as though he wanted to be sick and was fighting hard against it. In time, he might weaken, but time was one thing they didn't have.

"He don't know," Dixon announced angrily. "They ain't gonna trust no kid."

Russell Thurlow turned to stare at Todd Dixon, aware that his short-lived period of command was ending. Dixon jerked a thumb toward Sam Slagle. "He knows."

"Then make him talk, Sergeant." There was a note of defiance in Thurlow's tone that left the impression he didn't think Dixon was capable of making Slagle talk. At the same time, he was returning command of the operation to the renegade. Everyone recognized the situation for what it was.

"No." Dixon shook his head. He turned to look toward

Beth O'Roark, still huddled against the boulder. Her knees were drawn up, her head resting against them with her face hidden. At first glance, it looked as though she might be asleep, but there was a tenseness in her shoulders that showed she was listening.

"The girl's the one," Dixon declared. "Either she'll tell us." He glanced at Sam Slagle, jerking his chin at him. "Or he will before we're done with her." The meaning was plain. After all, Slagle had surrendered rather than have the girl harmed.

Thurlow stiffened at the realization of what Todd Dixon meant to do, but the renegade turned his back, glancing at one of his men. "Look over amongst them camels. They gotta have a coupla ropes."

"There's a dead Yankee over back of the camels," Rinker called after the man who went for the ropes. "Cover him up!"

Todd Dixon cast him a look of surprised disgust, but Rinker ignored it. Instead, he stalked to where Sid Jordan's bedroll lay and reached down to pull two blankets free. Without a glance at anyone, he dragged the blankets behind him until he reached the two troopers out of Able Smith's detail who had been killed in the battle. Without releasing his hold on his carbine, Rinker spread a blanket over each corpse.

Smith observed this pitiful ceremony with what had been a jaundiced expression at first, but as Rinker turned to walk past him, the trooper struggled up to a sitting position.

"Corporal Ringgold!"

Rinker paused to stare down at Smith, no change of expression showing in his features.

"Thanks," Smith muttered, suddenly embarrassed at commending an enemy. "They're my lads."

Rinker offered a tight nod and moved to the edge of

the clearing where he could observe, glancing thoughtfully in Beth O'Roark's direction once or twice.

If the girl knew she was under observation, she didn't indicate it by movement. Her face remained buried between her knees as though she was hiding from reality. Russell Thurlow, also watching her, wondered whether she had heard Todd Dixon's remarks. Probably not, he decided, or she would have reacted in some fashion.

Thurlow, himself, was pondering what Dixon had in mind for the girl. No matter what possibility he considered, he didn't like any of them. Dixon had shown himself to be little better than a rabid wolf. Any human emotions the man might once have known had been destroyed long ago.

The renegade leader holstered his clumsy pistol and strode across the sand-bottomed clearing to grab the girl by her shoulder and drag her to her feet. There was no struggle. Instead, Beth O'Roark simply stood there, shoulders slumped, head down so her eyes seemed to concentrate on the toes of her tormenter's boots.

"You know where that gold is, lady, you'd best tell me now," Dixon growled, then waited. If he expected a reaction, there was none. The girl simply stood there, as though she hadn't heard. Dixon stepped closer, shoving her head up so he could look into her face.

"You hear me, girl?"

"I hear." Her eyes were flat, looking a long way off, almost as though she was blind and searching for something she knew wasn't out there. Her voice was little more than a whisper. "I know nothing of any gold."

Dixon jerked his hand away and her head dropped, her eyes on the ground once more. For a moment, he seemed on the point of hitting her. Instead, he heaved a sigh of frustration. "It's on your head then, lady."

His man stood with two ropes he had scavenged from

the packing equipment. One was of hemp, the other a Mexican-made riata of plaited rawhide. Dixon grabbed the length of hemp, looping the lariat noose around the hands tied behind Beth O'Roark's back. She winced visibly as he jerked the noose tight.

For a moment she acted as though she would fight back, but the move was weak and half-hearted; a gesture, nothing more.

With the flat of his hand against her chest, Dixon shoved the girl back against the boulder where she had been sitting. Holding her firmly against the face of the big rock, he flipped the length of rope over the top, drawing it tight to pin her. The end of the rope, he tied around the girl's waist. She was firmly bound to the boulder.

"Leave her alone, dammit!" Slagle shouted. "She don't know nothin!"

Dixon seemed not to hear. He stepped closer to the girl, almost obscuring her figure with the bulk of his own body. Slagle turned his eyes upon Russell Thurlow. The officer stood as though dazed, not fully comprehending what he was seeing.

"Lootenant," Slagle demanded, "does the South 'spect to win by warrin' against women?" His words were loud. He wanted everyone to hear. "Is that your Southern way?"

Thurlow didn't stir. Instead, he continued to stare at Dixon and the girl. Then came the sound of tearing cloth and Dixon stepped back. The girl's head came up abruptly and a scream of outrage streamed from her lips. Her shirt had been ripped, almost torn off. Her shoulders, were exposed, white in the morning sun.

"Mother of God!" Slagle groaned. He struggled up to his knees, trying to rise, but a rifle butt in the hands of one of the renegades slammed his back into the sand.

Todd Dixon reached for the rawhide riata and uncoiled several feet of its length. In his hand, the length danced and writhed like a thin snake ready to strike, the heavy hide-reinforced loop in its end swinging back and forth like the reptile's head.

"Dixon! Stop!" Russell Thurlow stalked forward. "Drop that damned rope! Get back!"

Todd Dixon turned slowly, the rope clutched in his left hand. There was an odd, expectant smile on his lips, as he stared at the Confederate officer. The smile did not show in his eyes, which were slitted and watchful.

"We ain't got time to dally, soldier boy," he chided deliberately. "We gotta get that gold an' move outta here." He shifted his gaze to the distant horizon, offering a nod. "Injun smoke!"

Thurlow turned to look. Everyone did. Far off, perhaps twenty miles away, a single plume of white smoke rose into the sky, ultimately disintegrating in the upper breezes.

"I don't give a damn!" the officer declared, swinging back to face Dixon. But the renegade had taken advantage of the distraction. The LeMatt revolver was in his hand and he fired. Thurlow had been drawing his own sidearm as he turned. It had just cleared his holster. Now it dropped from his splayed fingers, as he was hurled backward by the full charge from the LeMatt's shotgun barrel.

"You outlived your uses, soldier boy." Dixon's tone held the same cruel, chiding note.

Russell Thurlow was on his back, blood from the wicked gut wound turning his shirt and the upper part of his pants scarlet. For an instant, he lay there, unable to comprehend. Then the pain struck with full force and he screamed. Dixon laughed, watching the dying Confederate writhe in the reddening sand.

Rinker had watched, motionless. Now he strode forward, dropping to his knees beside the young officer. Thurlow seemed to be babbling, talking to him in wild syllables, as his body jerked with spasms. Rinker listened, then drew his own revolver, jammed the muzzle against the man's temple, and fired. The shot echoed through the depression as the heavy-caliber bullet smashed into the lieutenant's skull. The body suddenly went limp, becoming a useless pile of blood-stained rags.

"Why'd you do that?" Dixon's complaint sounded like that of a disappointed child. Rinker's hand moved so that his revolver covered the renegade. He waited, daring Dixon to bring the big gun to bear. The latter realized what was happening. Carefully, he lowered the LeMatt's muzzle.

"He thought I was his grandfather," Rinker said softly, staring at Dixon. "He asked me to finish it.

"He also was a Confederate officer. He had a right to die with some dignity." There was a pause before Rinker added, "Something you wouldn't understand, Todd."

Dixon stared at Rinker for a moment, then carefully holstered his gun, turning back to the girl. He swung the length of plaited rawhide, judging where the heavy hondo would strike her to cause the most pain.

"And we *don't* war on women, Dixon. Cut her loose," Rinker ordered. Dixon froze, staring at him through those slitted eyes. "Now."

Dixon dropped the riata and slowly drew a knife from his belt. He sawed at the rope that held the girl, but was watching Rinker at the same time.

As the rope dropped away and the girl slumped, the renegade made his move. He dropped to the ground, hand clawing for the big gun. But there was no need.

A crude iron arrowhead had caught Rinker just above the ear. The man pitched forward on his face, the revolver dropping from his fingers.

An Apache war cry split the sudden silence.

Chapter Twenty-one

Before any of us could move, more rifle shots came from out in the desert. Two of the renegades, silhouetted against the skyline, fell and rolled down the incline toward where we were tied.

One of them rolled past, ending up in the bottom of the depression. The other's weight was caught against a small boulder and just hung there, the rock holding him at the waist, while his body sort of folded over it on both sides. Both men were dead.

"Beth!" I yelled. "Git in the hole!"

The girl had been staring at Rinker's body, I guess in shock at what she'd just seen. But at the sound of my voice, she looked up, sort of like a deer that's been startled while feeding.

"Git in the hole!" I yelled again, but this time, my voice was drowned out partly by Todd Dixon's yells.

"Get down. Get the hell under cover before your heads're blown off!" he shouted, charging toward the line of rocks. As he passed by me, I thrust out a foot to try to trip him, but he kicked me in the knee and kept going.

That hurt like hell and I thought for a second or so that

he'd broken my kneecap. But in the same moment, I saw that Beth had stopped to pick up something in the sand, then had jumped into the hole where the two of us'd been taken prisoner earlier.

"Th' stupid sonuvabitch hadda lead 'em right to us!" Sam Slagle snarled, looking up the incline to where Dixon was trying to organize his few remaining men into a ragged defense force.

Dixon grabbed two of the men by the back of their shirts, shoving them down in the sand on their faces, throwing their rifles on top of them. "Start shootin', dammit!" he roared.

Then he turned on two more of the outlaws, who were fumbling with their rifles, reloading. Apparently they had come into the camp with their longarms empty after shooting to distract us. Dixon gestured wildly toward the camels.

"You two! Get over there an' protect our backs." One of the men glanced up at him, not understanding. Dixon swung his boot, catching the man in the ribs. "Move it!"

Beside me, Sam Slagle was chuckling, watching all of this with what we used to call gallows humor. "First, he kills the best two men he's got an' now he starts kickin' the rest of 'em around. With luck, they may turn and kill him!"

I thought to point out to Sam that when I'd first joined his outfit, he'd put the boot to me once or twice to get my attention. But I understood the difference. His kick had been to impress me with my lack of camel education and the need to move faster. Todd Dixon was used to ruling by cruelty and didn't know no other way, even with his own men.

Half a dozen arrows arched down into the clearing, burying themselves part way in the sand. One of them were less than a foot from one of my boots. Without thinking, I pulled the leg closer to my body, trying to make a smaller target.

I was scared bad, but at the same time, I realized that, on the reverse slope of the rise as we were, we prisoners were protected better than Dixon's men on the firing line. At least, that's what I thought for that moment. Then there were more arrows raining down on us. It was almost as though the Apaches didn't really know where we were located in the little clearing, but felt that, with enough saturation, they'd take some of us out. And they were right.

There was a cry of pain and anger and I rolled over on my back to look. Able Smith had been lying on his belly, hands tied behind him so he could look uphill and see what was happening. An arrow had caught him right between the shoulder blades, as it had descended, the iron battle head burying itself in his body. He kicked and cried out for a couple of seconds, then relaxed, either dead or unconscious.

I looked away to see that one of the two men Dixon had started across the clearing hadn't made it. He was down, crawling across the sand toward the hole where Beth was hidden. His blood was leaving a red trail in the sand behind him. Several arrows also had been buried half their length in the closest camel and it was down, kicking out the final moments of its life.

Sam Slagle had used his body as a pivot to turn half way around so he could look up the hill.

"Dixon! Hear me, dammit! Turn us loose so we can fight!"

The renegade didn't bother to look up from where he was reloading one of the carbines that had belonged to a dead man.

"Cut us loose an' let us help!" Slagle called again, his tone rising to a scream of frustration. He had known he could die at the hands of renegades, Rebels or Apaches all the time he'd been leading the camel caravans, but he never had thought his life would end groveling in the sand with his hands tied behind his back, waiting for that stray shot that would kill him.

"You might as well cut us loose, 'cause you ain't leavin here!" Slagle blazed at him. "That smoke signal was from a cavalry detachment that's been keepin' track of us. They're on th' way right now. If the Injuns don't getcha, our troopers will!"

This was the first I had known about any such plan and I took it as a desperate lie. We both watched as Dixon turned to glance to where he had stashed our weapons in that cleft in the rocks. Sam Slagle's six-shot Colt carbine was among those arms and some of the Dragoons probably had full cylinders.

Dixon said something curtly to one of his men. The renegade glanced at him, then down at the man who had been crawling in the sand. He was still now, blood pooling beneath him and seeping out to color the sand.

The renegade seemed on the point of refusing, but finally shrugged. He handed Dixon his carbine and half rose to his feet, keeping as low as he could. He ran down the hill, but instead of making for the arms cache, he ran in among the camels that were still on their feet milled about something frightful, trying to break loose from where we had them tied. After a minute, I saw what he was about. He was checking packs and saddlebags for extra loaded cylinders, throwing uniforms and personal gear about.

It had always been our practice to carry with us extra cylinders loaded with powder and ball. That way, if we got in a fight, we could switch cylinders without having to take the time to reload.

The man found the extra cylinders and stuffed them all

into Slagle's saddlebags, swinging the load across his shoulder. He was well weighed down, but managed to stagger past the hole where Beth was hidden, reaching into the arms cache and gathering up several carbines and Colt Dragoons pistols. Slagle's prized rifle was among them.

The man couldn't carry all of the guns, so he grabbed up a piece of the rope that had bound Beth O'Roark earlier. He hunkered down to feed the rope through the trigger guards, stringing them like beads on a thread. When he had all he figured he could drag, he grabbed both ends of the rope and started toward us, the guns furrowing the sand behind him.

A couple of Dixon's men ran down to help him drag the guns up past us. When he saw what treatment his Colt revolving carbine was taking, Sam Slagle swore with a verve that must have made God cover his ears.

Then Dixon was on his knees beside me. He fumbled for his knife, but it wasn't in his sheath. He scowled, then reached down to claw with the knots that tied my hands. He finally was able to get me free.

During all this, Slagle had been watching expectantly. "Come on," he urged. "Hurry it up." He was expecting to be freed to fight, but Dixon didn't even look at him.

"You're gonna load for us," Dixon told me. "Make one move that ain't gun-loadin' an' I'll kill yuh!"

I sat there, the blood running into my fingers, feeling the hurt. I glanced at Slagle, but he already had figured out what Dixon wanted. I was the only one he would turn loose. I didn't know what to do. If I joined them, it was like desertion to the enemy. If I didn't, Todd Dixon would kill me. Slagle saw the puzzlement and confusion in my eyes. Lying on his side, he nodded with a scowl.

"Do what he says, Corporal. That's an order."

I was ashamed at how I felt and hoped it didn't show

in my face. I was relieved to be freed. Happy to be able to do something besides just lie there waiting for them arrows to make me into an Apache pin cushion. Taking care not to look at Slagle, not wanting him to see my eagerness, I rolled over on my hands and knees and scrambled up into the rocks, Todd Dixon close behind me.

As I settled in amongst the rocks, Dixon shoved several carbines and revolvers at me. The saddlebags full of cylinders were thrown at my feet. I opened them and saw that, besides the loaded cylinders, there was a supply of powder, lead balls, primers and a can of beef tallow.

My hands were shaking, but I began to load the empty guns.

Once, pouring powder into the bore of a carbine, I looked up to where Dixon had positioned himself. I pondered the chances of shooting him, but he was angled in such a way, firing Slagle's six-shooter carbine between a cleft in the rocks, that he could well see any untoward move I made out of the corner of his eye. That big old pistol was right beside him, where it could be grabbed up in a hurry to blow me to kingdom come. He was figuring way ahead of me.

Besides, if I killed him, that would be one less to fight off the Apaches. There was no way I could shoot him, get down the hill and cut Slagle and the others loose without the other renegades killing me.

There was nothing I could do but keep loading their guns.

Chapter Twenty-two

I don't know how long I hunkered there, going through the motions, pouring measures of powder down the muzzle of a carbine, ramming a bullet down on top of it, then pinching the little copper primer on the nipple, handing the gun upward. Someone would grab it and hand me another empty longarm.

And after the extra cylinders had been shot up, there were the revolvers. Each cylinder had to have powder measured into each of the six chambers, then a ball rammed down on top of each of the charges. Finally, I dug into the tin of tallow and smeared grease over the end of each chamber. That was to prevent a chain fire. Sometimes, if the chamber wasn't sealed that way, a spark from the one that was fired could set off the other chambers in a roar of gunpowder that could destroy the gun and probably the hand holding it. Again, a primer was pinched onto each of the nipples, one for each chamber.

Todd Dixon handed me down Sam Slagle's Colt carbine several times and maybe I took a bit more care with it than I did the others. If we ever got out of this and Sam found I'd been careless enough to damage his pet shootin' stick, he'd kill me on the spot, I figured.

Dixon kept the big LeMatt pistol close beside him, seeming to want to save it. Once, though, when the firing got right heavy and I hadn't finished reloading the Colt carbine, he fired all the rounds in the LeMatt and handed it down to me. Like with Slagle's carbine, I took extra pains with Dixon's big LeMatt. Special pains.

I didn't know exactly when it happened each time, but more of Dixon's outlaws died there in that jumble of rocks, and the firing on our side was growing less frequent.

Then, suddenlike, the shooting by the Apaches stopped. At first, I was so busy loading I didn't notice. Then Dixon stopped firing, listening. Nothing. Just a silence that was hard to recognize for what it was.

"Must be Cap'n Wright an' his troopers're comin'," Slagle called from where he was tied. I glanced down toward him and was full of horror at what was there. Slagle was the only one of our band alive besides myself. The others were dead from arrows or gunfire. Beyond, where the camels were tied, looked like a slaughterhouse. Everyone of the animals was down except for Big Red.

Laying down the gun I had been loading, I crept up into the rocks, shoving a dead renegade out of the way so I could see. There was no sign of an Indian. If there had been dead, the Apaches seemed to have taken them away, though how it could be achieved with all that firing was hard to figure.

Then there came a shrill, arrogant cry and I saw a string of horsemen ride up over a sand dune, driving the horses that must have belonged to Dixon's men. They weren't leaving with our scalps, but they had something to show for their raid. They might keep several of the good mounts. The rest they'd probably eat, if I knew anything about Apaches.

Dixon leveled Slagle's carbine, squinting down the sights and fired. The Indians were well out of range and the bullet kicked up sand a hundred yards short. Dixon cursed and turned to where I was hunkered. He swung the muzzle of the carbine toward me and pulled the trigger. The hammer clicked on an empty cylinder.

Throwing the carbine down, he clawed for the LeMatt which lay in the sand near his knee, starting to bring it up.

"You still ain't got the gold, Dixon." My heart was in my mouth and I hoped he took in what I was saying before he thumbed the trigger. The shotgun barrel was empty, I knew, but the other cylinders were loaded. He was closer than I wanted.

Dixon hesitated, glaring at me through sun-reddened eyes, but I was staring past him, eyeing the desert. A long way off there was a line of what seemed to be haze that stretched across the whole horizon. I recognized why the Apaches had pulled out.

"You're all alone," I told him, "an you still ain't got what you come after. You ain't got a horse neither."

"Wagner! Shut your damned mouth!" Dixon shouted at me.

"You know where that gold is, boy?" Slagle growled at me, the LeMatt revolver's bore centered on my chest. I hesitated, then nodded.

"That I do. Under the dead Injun scout." I avoided Slagle's glare. When I'd helped him cover the body, my hand struck the keg he had shoved under the body. I'd known all along where he had it hid.

Slagle was cussing me for a traitor, while Dixon waved the muzzle of the big gun at me. "Get up. Without a gun!"

I rose slowly, taking care to keep my hands away from

the guns that surrounded me. Several of them were fully loaded. I knew which ones.

Dixon heaved himself to his feet from where he'd been hunkered and motioned again with the gun. "Let's get the gold."

I stumbled down the incline, staying clear of Slagle. Crossing the bottom of the little depression, I angled toward the outcropping that had helped protect us. I glanced once toward the hole where Beth O'Roark was hidden, but I couldn't see her. I wondered, anxious-like, whether she was still alive or if maybe she had been hit by a stray bullet or an arrow.

I cut around the outcropping and waded across the open sand toward the spot where Slagle and I had buried the dead Apache scout. When we reached the spot, I wasn't surprised to find the sand dug up, signs of moccasin tracks only partly covered by blowing sand. The Indians had backtracked and found the shallow grave, too. I dug down into the sand, then stopped.

"What's wrong?" Todd Dixon demanded behind me.

"The body's gone," I told him.

"What about the gold?" He was close now and had the muzzle of the LeMatt against the back of my neck. I was on my knees, feeling around in the sand, digging deeper till I felt it. In their rush to take the body away, the Apaches had missed the iron-bound keg or, more likely, hadn't cared about it. I felt its hard roundness beneath the loose sand and began to dig it out with my hands. Finally, I was able to roll it free.

Dixon had backed away from me, never the careless type even if excited about the gold. I'd thought of throwing sand in his face and trying to take the big pistol, but I reckoned he'd thought about the same thing.

"Pick it up!" Dixon ordered and watched, revolver leveled on my belt buckle, as I struggled to get the heavy cask on my shoulder. Bowed beneath it, I staggered through the sand back to the camp.

Slagle was standing now, but his hands still were tied behind his back. He glanced around him, his expression one of unending sadness at the sight of the dead men, the troopers he had known so well. He turned to look at me, as I staggered into the enclave and dropped the keg in the sand. His expression of sadness didn't change. He just shook his head and turned his back on me to move from one dead trooper to the next.

Dixon paused, giving Slagle a long look, then turned his piggish red eyes back to me. He indicated the keg with a wave of his gun muzzle. "I want to see it."

I wasn't sure what he meant.

"I want to see the gold!" he snarled. "Smash it!"

I picked up a big rock and brought it down on the head of the keg, splintering the wood. The glint of gold pieces showed underneath. Dixon bent to pick up several of them, rubbing them in his hand, staring at them.

Then he shoved them back into the keg, stepping back to wave the gun muzzle at me once more. "Tie something over it."

Using the Bowie knife that hung on Slagle's saddle to cut a piece of canvas from one of the packs, I covered the head of the cask with the heavy cloth. The rawhide riata lay in the dust and I sliced off a length to tie the canvas cover in place. Then I straightened and glanced at Dixon, knowing what was coming next.

"Sam!" I called. "Stay away from them guns or he'll kill you. They're all empty anyhow."

Slagle had been edging toward the spot where I'd been reloading the array of arms. He stopped and turned toward us. Dixon was watching him, the LeMatt's muzzle pointed in his direction. The renegade offered a nasty chuckle.

"Good advice, boy. You'll all be dead soon enough. Get that camel out here an' get a saddle on it!"

I cast another glance at Slagle and winked at him before I turned away. The sergeant looked surprised, then offered a lowering of his chin, as though to say it was my play.

I led Big Red out and slung the camel saddle up onto her back, cinching it down as tight as I could. Dixon had been struggling into one of Slagle's uniform shirts, that had been scattered in the hunt for loaded cylinders. He picked up a cavalry hat and jammed it down on his head. Then he motioned me back with the gun, while he checked the saddle rigging. He was going to try to pass himself off as a Union survivor!

"Now make her lie down so's I can get on," he ordered.

I tapped the camel across the knees and she dropped down onto them with a protesting grunt. She swung her head to offer Dixon a baleful look and I couldn't help smiling, though I turned my head to hide it.

Still holding the gun on me, Dixon climbed clumsily into the saddle and settled himself. Then he nodded.

"Now the gold!"

I struggled to lift the keg and staggered with it to where he sat astride the camel. I balanced it across the saddle in front of him. At the same time, I signaled the camel to get up on its feet.

That was the moment when Beth O'Roark came out of the hole, a knife in her hand. It was the blade Dixon had used to cut her loose from the boulder. Screaming like a banshee, she hurled herself straight at Todd Dixon.

I must have been screaming, too, as I threw myself in front of her. The LeMatt roared as Dixon pulled the trigger, then there was another scream, a sound of pain and fear. Part of his hand was blown away and fragments of metal from the barrel had shattered his face.

Some of the exploding steel must have struck the camel, too, for it began to run, going straight up over the rocks, while Dixon tried to hang on with his good hand. The wooden cask fell and shattered in the rocks.

I ran then, charging up the incline to where the rifles and revolvers lay. I picked up a carbine I knew was loaded. Todd Dixon, by some superhuman means, was clinging to the back of the camel. I raised the carbine, found the sights and aligned them with his retreating back.

A big hand grabbed the fore end of the carbine, forcing it down. My shot ricocheted into the rocks in front of us.

I tried to wrestle the carbine away from Slagle, but he held it firm. He wasn't looking at me. He was staring out across the desert. The leather thongs still encircled his wrists, but they had been neatly sliced between by Beth and her knife. Dixon was out of range and Big Red was still running. Beyond them was that band of yellowish haze I'd seen earlier. But the sandstorm was closer now.

"I want the desert to get the devil!" Slagle said quietly.

Epilogue

That sandstorm was drawing closer and we watched it sweep over Big Red and her rider, blotting them out. We ran back to grab a big tarp and, with Beth O'Roark, all three of us crowded into that hole, covering ourselves with the canvas, as best we could.

The storm came howling in, tearing at the canvas sheet, while we tried to keep covered. Still, the sand blowed in around the corners to near suffocate us. I don't know how long it all lasted, but between struggling to keep breathing and trying to blot out of my mind all that'd happened, I came to recognize I wasn't cut out to be a professional soldier.

I'd trusted Sam Slagle and he'd double-crossed me. Maybe it was orders from Captain Wright that he shouldn't tell me the full truth of what was going on, but it was my life they had gambled with. If I was going to die as a soldier, I should at least have full knowledge of why.

I'd come to know the whole thing was a trap when that cask fell off Big Red's saddle and smashed on the rocks. There wasn't more than a thousand dollars in gold coins stuffed in each end of that keg for the sake of appearance. In between the layers was nothing but a lot of lead washers to give the keg the weight of gold.

That was full disillusionment for me and I guess I didn't take my soldiering all that serious from then on. Being used for bait wasn't my idea of any profession I wanted to follow for another twenty or thirty years.

After the storm passed, Slagle and me piled up some dry brush from what grew there in that little enclave and lit it off. That was supposed to have been the signal for Captain Wright and his troops to ride in and capture the renegades, Slagle said, but we'd never had a chance to signal it like was planned.

We was a lot worse for wear and Beth O'Roark was nigh onto being a mental case before we finally all got to Fort Yuma.

A burial detail was sent back from there to bring in the bodies of the troopers. We'd covered them as best we could and Captain Wright left some men to guard the remains against varmints, buzzards, and maybe Indian looters.

I still wake up some nights, sweating over the memory of all the good men who died in that shallow hole amongst the rocks. Able Smith, Sid Jordan. Even that wet-eared Rebel officer and the deserter that called himself Rinker. They'd been good men, too, in their way. At least, both had showed a sense of honor in the end.

It would be nice to say I married Beth O'Roark and we lived happily ever after. That didn't happen. She'd had a bellyful of the frontier West, I reckon, and caught the first stagecoach headed back East to Boston. She had to wait a time and I seen her around Fort Yuma a time or two while Slagle and me was recovering our health and she was waiting for passage, but she didn't seem the least interested in talking about what happened, so I didn't say much to her.

It might even be nice to be able to say she married Sam Slagle, but he was in love with the U.S. Cavalry. When I complained about the way I'd been kept in the dark so I could die stupid, he just shrugged and said that as soldiers, we didn't really have a right to know what was happening. We were just to do as we were told.

I got over wanting to kill all the Johnny Rebs in the world and I was right happy to sit out the rest of the war with the guard detachment at the Presidio in San Francisco.

It wasn't long after that the federal government give up on the idea of a camel corps and most of them animals was taken to some base down in the California coast, where they spent the rest of the war eating and being generally dangerous to anyone that came near them. After the war, I heard some was sold off to be worked in the Nevada mines and others was just turned loose in the desert.

I got my discharge and tried a whole passel of things to make a living before I got into the hotel business. Once, when matters wasn't going too good, I wrote to that author fellow, Ned Buntline. He's the one who wrote all that trash about Buffalo Bill Cody and Wild Bill Hickok and made them famous.

I figured, if he'd write one of his Penny Dreadfuls about what happened to us out there in the Mojave, I might get to be just as famous as those two and maybe make some money.

I never did hear from him, though. Either he never got my letter or he figured no one would believe that sort of tale. No one else ever did, when I tried to talk about it. Finally, I just shut up and quit making a fool of myself.

As for Sam Slagle, I don't really know what ever become of him. As soon as we was returned to duty, he wrangled a transfer to some horse soldier outfit back East, where he could fight the war for serious.

I heard he got hisself killed in one of the late campaigns, but I never was able to learn the real truth about it. I suppose I might have written the War Department to maybe learn something about what become of him, but I just never seemed to get around to it.

When I had stuffed sand and tallow into the barrel of Dixon's LeMatt, I'd expected the blow-up to kill him outright. As for Big Red, I always knew that ugly creature would come to a bad end. With her personality made up of whole poison, her and Todd Dixon sort of deserved each other.

The moon was low in the sky and the big red camel was worn and staggering by the time the band of Yaquis finally cornered her in a box canyon. They had heard about such strange creatures, but none of them had seen one before.

The braves were surprised to find the man in the horse soldier uniform clinging to her back, more dead than alive. He was delirious and kept muttering about gold. He sat there in the deep saddle, clutching his ruined hand that was festering with gangrene, staring out of blind, sightless eyes.

When he wasn't talking about gold, he laughed at his captors even though he couldn't see them. He muttered things that sounded like "Thurlow" and " Rinker" and "Yankee buzzards" but the sounds didn't mean anything. All of the braves knew he was crazy and a crazy man demanded respect and even a bit of fear. The demons had taken over his mind. It wouldn't do to have those demons transfer their being to your own mind in a fit of anger.

That was cause enough for the vague fears all the Yaquis felt, deep inside.

There were the young bucks, showing off with false bravado, who wanted to kill the madman and eat the camel, but the older braves said the big animal was just as crazy as the rider on its back. It tried to bite anyone who ventured close to its head or it would lash out with one of those cloven hooves that could break a man's leg.

Finally there was a compromise. While two of the braves held the angry, vicious animal by its halter, two more used rawhide strips, wet and stretched in water, to tie the man's legs under the beast's belly. That would ensure that the man and his demons would not come back to haunt them. He would travel into The Darkness on the back of the camel, never to bother the Yaquis or their children.

With the knots firmly tied and the rawhide already starting to shrink in the dry night air, the halter was released. The animal, pained by the tightness of the rawhide under its belly, squealed in frustration and lashed out at the braves with teeth and hooves. It should have been a moment for jokes and laughter, but the Yaquis suddenly were fearful of what they had done. They might have angered the demons even more.

Quickly the Indians rode away, scattering in several directions. Then they turned their horses atop the Mojave sand dunes to watch as the camel broke into a trot and disappeared into the night.

The only sound that drifted back was the crazed laughter of her rider.